Acclaim for Chielozona Eze's

THE TRIAL OF ROBERT MUGABE

"A new novel that depicts the fictional trial of Zimbabwean leader Robert Mugabe."

—*BBC World Service*

"The service of The Trial of Robert Mugabe to Zimbabwe's collective healing should not be undervalued. The scenario of the novel is as urgent as it is sceptical."

—*Pambazuka News*

"The Trial of Robert Mugabe is a valuable and easy read. The events of the legal proceedings flow smoothly and Eze ultimately presents an optimistic message: that justice in Africa is part of universal notions of justice and will ultimately triumph."

—*African Arguments*

"Eze's The Trial of Robert Mugabe, explicitly regards 'postcolonial fever' as a malady afflicting contemporary African societies and cultures that precludes justice rather than furthering it."

—*Postcolonial Justice*

"A Nigerian writer's blend of fictionalized eyewitness accounts of murderous repression, political satire, and philosophical essay that not only exposes the disastrous consequences of Mugabe's regime for Zimbabwean society, but also explores the significance of the political ideology generated by that regime in a pan-African setting."

—*Engaging with Literature of Commitment*

Chielozona Eze

THE TRIAL OF ROBERT MUGABE

Chielozona Eze is a Nigerian writer and philosopher. He studied Catholic theology, philosophy and literature, creative writing in Nigeria, Austria, Germany and the US. He is a Stellenbosch Fellow and the recipient of the Olaudah Equiano Prize for African Fiction. He teaches Postcolonial African Literature at Northeastern Illinois University, Chicago.

ALSO BY CHIELOZONA EZE

Poetry

Prayers to Survive Wars that Last
Survival Kit

Essays

Race, Decolonization, and Global Citizenship in South Africa

Ethics and Human Rights in Anglophone African
Women's Literature: Feminist Empathy

Postcolonial Imaginations and Moral Representations
in African Literature and Culture

The Dilemma of Ethnic Identity: Alain Locke's Vision
of Transcultural Societies

The Trial
of Robert Mugabe

CWP

The Trial of Robert Mugabe

Chielozona Eze

CWP

v

Published 2019
Cissus World Press
Milwaukee, Wisconsin

Library of Congress Cataloging-in-Publication Data

Chielozona Eze
The Trial of Robert Mugabe

ISBN: 978-1-7335872-1-1
1. Zimbabwe–Fiction. 2. History–Fiction. 3. African Dictatorship–Fiction. 4. Human Rights Abuse–Fiction.

Cover photo: "Hope" by Dike Okoro

To the memory of
Yvonne Vera and Dambudzo Marechera
And All Souls, Zimbabwe, 1980-2009

Those who are picked for trial are sometimes just symbols of wider phenomena.

Ali Mazrui, *The Trial of Christopher Okigbo*

We would rather be ruined than change
We would rather die in our dread
Than climb the cross of the Present
And let our illusions die.

W. H. Auden, "Age of Anxiety"

Part One

The Voice of the People
2000-2008

In God's Court

Robert Mugabe, dressed in his quaint army uniform, sat between two brawny soldiers. Three other soldiers sat behind him; the palms of their hands were placed on their knees, their gazes stonily fixed to the front. He did not understand what was happening, but since the soldiers were his bodyguards, he saw no reason to panic. Not yet. But as soon as the other section of the court began to fill up, his calm gave way to misgivings. First to appear was Joshua Nkomo, followed by Bishop Abel Muzorewa, Ndabaningi Sithole, and Joshua Gumede. Mugabe's face tightened in distress. He gnashed his teeth, scratched at his tiny Hitler mustache and leaned to his left. "What's going on here?" he asked the soldier on that side.

"What, your excellency?" the soldier inquired, taken aback by Mugabe's question.

Mugabe pointed in the direction of Nkomo. "What are they doing here?"

"Oh, your excellency, they have come to the trial," the soldier answered.

"The trial? Whose trial?"

The soldier looked back at the others, who exchanged glances among themselves. Could it be that Mugabe was the only person in that hall who didn't know why he was there? In the end, the soldier immediately behind him had the courage to tell him. "It is your trial, your excellency," he said.

"What?" he asked in a furious tone of voice. "My trial? Who on earth can have me on trial?"

"The people," the soldier on his right whispered in an attempt to calm him down. "God," the other said.

"Who? People? God?" Mugabe asked nervously.

"*Vox populi, vox Dei,* your excellency," the first soldier said.

Mugabe stared at the soldier, still frowning. How could such daring words come out of his mouth? The soldier nevertheless knew what he was saying. He had the opportunity to glimpse the audience, whose testimony would constitute the bulk of the trial. Mugabe hadn't seen them because a thick curtain separated him from the people. He looked around nervously. Patches of clouds raced by

3

a few meters below him. "Where are we?" he asked. "How did we get here?"

"We're in God's court," the soldier on his left said, pointing to the big throne about twenty meters from them, covered with a long, pale, filmy curtain. The edges of the throne could be discerned. A human-like figure sat there. It could well have been a human, but one couldn't be sure. One expected some kind of movement from it, something like a yawn, a scratch of the eyebrow, a sneeze, or an attempt to adjust its sitting position. None came. Behind the throne was the dark blue one saw in the summer mornings in West African skies. Behind Nkomo's section, there was a blue drape, and one behind Mugabe. These drapes were transparent; one could see plainly human figures moving about, who appeared to be floating in the air. Their voices were so distinct that one could understand them with only minimal effort. Right at the center of the stage was a long table, on which three microphones were placed. In front of the microphones were name plates that read *Steve Biko, Olaudah Equiano,* and *Dambudzo Marechera.* On the right side of the middle microphone was a wooden gavel.

"So this is God's court," Mugabe said in a subdued voice. "Am I dead?"

"Yes, your excellency," the soldier on his right answered gently. "You've been dead for some time."

"You died in a plane crash, your excellency," the one sitting directly behind him said.

"Plane crash? How could I have a plane crash without knowing? What are you telling me?"

"Your excellency," the one on his left went on, "you remember we attended the summit of African heads of state. The African Union. It happened after that summit, your excellency. The pilot reported some mechanical problems before we took off from Cairo International Airport, so the plane had to be repaired. It took some time to get repaired, but we finally took off. Just as we were in the middle of Sahara Desert, the pilot reported that the problem had recurred and it was worse. He announced that we were going down. It was then that you fainted."

"Okay," he said, in a tone of surprising acquiescence. "Is he black?" he asked, pointing at the throne. "No white God will ever preside over my trial."

4

The soldier didn't answer. Neither did any of the others. The question was obviously beyond their knowledge. But hardly had Mugabe asked his last question when the judges strode into the hall. The first, a relatively young, man with a Rasta, took his position: Dambudzo Marechera. The second man was pronouncedly tall, but less robust. He had full hair, carefully coiffured in an old-fashioned manner and parted at the left side; he wore a *kente* wraparound cloth slung over his left shoulder: Olaudah Equiano. The third, tall and slim, with a patchy beard, wore a white shirt and a casual brown coat over dark blue trousers: Steve Biko.

When they took their positions behind their nameplates, the curtain separating the two sections of the court gradually pulled back. Uncountable pairs of eyes instinctively turned to the left, and, like magnets to iron, latched on to Mugabe. Thousands of white and black faces–children, youth, men, women–all mixed together: black people of different skin hues, some as dark as charcoal, others as light as ripe banana. Some had faces as long as Benin masks. Others had faces like happy Zulu war dancers. Most people looked very lean and haggard, but shadows of smiles hovered over their lips while their eyes glittered with curiosity. For now, however, the sight of Robert Gabriel Mugabe appeared to have transfixed them.

Mugabe recognized many faces there and grew nervous. He recognized Shona faces, Ndebele faces, white faces and faces he couldn't quite place, although he remembered seeing them at least once. He had seen them die of hunger, or beaten to death by the members of the Fifth Brigade. He had laughed to himself when white people were being driven out of their farms, some of their women raped; he had heard these people's groans and thought they deserved their fate. But now, now in God's court, what have these people to say? What stories have they to tell?

When he glanced at the end of the first pew on the right and saw Yvonne Vera, standing behind a big Minolta camera recording the event, his nervousness became more pronounced. Yvonne calmly pushed back a strand of her braids behind her left ear and, directed the camera to him. Then she stood aside; since Mugabe could not easily avert his eyes. His stomach felt hollow and cold as Yvonne's eyes bore into his. If he hadn't realized what the trial was

5

about before, he now knew. It was his nemesis, the mass killings in Matabeleland. He had read her novel, *The Stone Virgins,* and knew she had been afraid to accuse him before the world. She, like other Zimbabwean writers, obviously feared for her life back then. But now that all of them were before God, she would surely not hide anything. She would tell it as it was.

But Mugabe wasn't the type who yielded to self-pity. No, such a thing wasn't in his nature. Instead, he shrugged his shoulders, controlled his tension and braced himself for whatever would come. He would surely defend himself, he thought, and God would understand. If he were an African God, he certainly would. He adjusted the green-and-yellow-striped shawl that hung from his left shoulder, across his chest, pinned at his right hip. He ran his left hand over its inscription, "Freedom Fighter," as though to assure himself that it would save him. And just as he did, a big drum boomed, a trumpet sounded and a soft flute crooned a prelude for a warm voice that rang out in a well-known song: "Nkosi Sikelel' iAfrika." Every person in the hall stood and sang with verve.

Nkosi Sikelel' iAfrika
Maluphakanyisw' uphondo lwayo
Yiva imathandazo yethu
Nkosi Sikelela
Thina lusapho lwayo

Lord, bless Africa
May her spirit rise high up
Hear thou our prayers
Lord bless us.

When the song ended, about 20 figures sauntered toward the stage; they walked on the air, enjoying their weightlessness. They were a mix of people of different ethnic backgrounds. Two of them were most visible; their noses literally touched the right drape, so their profiles were very distinct. As were their words: *"Bestimmt sind sie Afrikaner."* *"Ja, Afrikaner. Sie warten auf den Weltgeist."*

For the first time since Mugabe and Yvonne's eyes met, Yvonne smiled, obviously happy that the Pan-African national hymn attracted the attention of these two Germans. But as much as her face lit up, Mugabe's darkened. He, too, saw the two white people, understood what they said. That, indeed, made his case worse. *Weltgeist*! Wasn't this an all-African affair? What had *Weltgeist* to do with Africans? Does it then mean that people from other parts of the world could hear what was going to be said about him?

The people sat back after the song; when they had settled, the Chief Judge, Olaudah Equiano, stood up and welcomed all to that month's trial, the last trial before summer break. He especially welcomed Yvonne Vera, whose accounts of the mass execution of Ndebeles in Matabeleland would be of immense importance to today's trial. He announced that Enoch Sontonga, whose song they all had joyously sung, would remind them of the protocols and due process of African Afterlife trials. He stretched his right hand in a welcoming gesture to a man in his early 70s, sitting in the first position on the first pew on the left side.

Enoch Sontonga, tall and robust, was dressed in a slightly worn but perfectly ironed suit that made him look like a colonial native administrator. He stepped forward and bowed slightly to the throne. He turned to the three judges and thanked them for making him today's announcer, an honor he would never forget. He had witnessed many trials of African leaders, he said, but this one was special to him for the very reason that Zimbabwe and South Africa shared common historical traits. "Like our writer said in her book, from which we shall hear more today," he said as he grandly swept his right hand in Yvonne's direction. "*Selborne is the most splendid street in Bulawayo, and you can look down it for miles and miles…Selborne carries you straight out of the city limits and head all the way to Johannesburg, like an umbilical cord.*"

The people applauded the lines that Sontonga recited in the right poetic cadence. Yvonne was visibly touched. She closed her eyes, enjoying the applause and the appreciation of the many who turned in her direction. Sontonga went on with his address, hinting he was sure that if the good people of South Africa did not check their dangerous path of resentment, South Africa might be herded into the same condition Zimbabwe was.

"Wasteland!" shouted a voice from the audience.

Sontonga turned to the person who shouted—a lean black man in his early 30s. Many eyes turned to the man, who still whispered to himself: *Wasteland, wasteland, nothing grows there any longer*. The white woman seated to his left nudged him with her elbow. He stopped.

The day's trial, Enoch went on, was of importance to South Africa, which also had a flourishing white minority like Zimbabwe. Africa had been a home of despots and mass killings. As Africans, they wished no more than that all these brutalities stop. They were concerned that life has ceased to thrive on that continent; they were eager for it to begin to flourish regardless of where the inspiration came from.

Sontonga looked up and, seeing no obvious sign of enthusiasm for his long speech, shrugged it off and glanced at the piece of paper in his left hand. "Fellow Africans of the Afterlife," he went on, "we have come here to tell stories and not to judge any person. We do this with the knowledge that the evils that men do live after them."

There were smiles on people's faces. He nodded his head with satisfaction, knowing that he had struck the right chord. "Yes, brothers and sisters," he went on. "We tell stories to keep good deeds alive. But we also want to make sure that the living and the dead hear about their deeds and judge themselves. If they can't judge themselves, as many of us are surely incapable of doing, the Ultimate Judge, the Eternal One, whose verdict we are bound to respect, will pass on judgment."

He lowered his voice for effect. "Not one of us is above that judgment. Yet it is not ours to judge. *Judge not lest ye be judged.* Isn't that the case?"

"Yes, brother, it is," voices responded in near unison. Yvonne briefly turned the camera to Mugabe, who stared like a statue.

"Yes," Mr. Sontonga went on. "We are going to hear stories of how we met our deaths. We Africans have not always had it easy, but we have always borne our misery stoically, knowing that a day like this will come, a day on which even the dumb will find his voice and the blind will find his eyes."

He smiled to himself, happy with his metaphor. "The crippled will find his legs and walk distances."

"Run distances," a voice added jovially, attracting some chuckles and

8

applause.

"Yes, bro," he said. "I therefore call on the first witness to share his or her experience with us. Story, and nothing but story," he emphasized.

But just as Sontonga was about to withdraw to his position, Joshua Nkomo stood up. "I thank you, sir, for this great African introduction," he said. "This is a trial. No trial goes without accusation. I therefore stand here to formally accuse Robert Gabriel Mugabe of *Guku Africanus*. I am here to say loud and clear, *J'accuse*."

Joshua Nkomo's booming voice sent a chilling silence through the audience. People looked around, caught unaware by the directness of his language. What was he doing? And *Guku Africanus*? What, in the name of Mama Africa, could that be? They have always known that he was an elite, intent on keeping his distance from common folks.

Footnote #1

Guku Africanus? It's a difficult term to define. The first thing to know, however, is that Zimbabweans knew it as *Gukurahundi*, or cleansing. It is a Shona word meaning the first rain of the season that cleanses the earth of chaff and dirt.

That is the original meaning, but, as our dear readers would attest, over time, words acquire more meanings than originally intended. So, the current and most important meaning of *Guku Africanus* is that it is a curse, the original African curse, a *juju* hovering over the African sky whose potency lies in the fact that it intoxicates the African mind, especially that of their leaders. When the spirit of *Guku* possesses an African leader, he feels like a famished vampire. These are some of the most outstanding symptoms: His heart knocks on his rib cage like a boy throwing tantrums; his breath becomes overly labored; his nose flares, his lips itch and burn and he licks them. Only fresh blood can douse the hotness of those lips. Blood! Pure and innocent African blood. And just like an intoxicated bee never flies off a cup of palm wine, these African leaders simply bathe in blood; they wriggle in the blood of their people like hyena kids wriggle and bathe in a decaying carcass.

It is perhaps important to note that *Guku* spirit is not peculiar to Africa,

9

although African leaders appear too eager to claim it as their birthright. Nero, it was said, was possessed by a *Guku* that made him whine like a bitch in heat until Rome was in ashes. We choose to identify his as *Guku Romanus*. Hitler had a *Guku Teutonicus* and his heart wouldn't beat normally until he sent millions of Jews to their deaths. Europeans have lots of stories to tell in this regard, a lot of *Gukus*. Not long ago, Milosevic demonstrated the same lust for blood in Bosnia-Herzegovina. And the Americas have too. Africa has as many *Gukus* as one is ready to remember. We easily remember these: the *Guku Nigerianus*, the *Guku Rwandanus*, the *Guku Ugandanus*, the *Guku Sierra Leonis, Guku Somalis* etc.

All of these African *Gukus* and many more, share the same characteristic: they resist rational explanation. They defy why. *Gukus* always defy explanation. Has anyone successfully explained the holocaust? Not until we can explain why Cain killed Abel. At any rate, since not everything lends itself to rational explanation, and since we cannot do justice to the why of *Guku*, we, imperfect vessels of the gods, resort to stories if only to show how.

The Terrible Journey of Emerson Manyika

The silence that trailed Nkomo's words, *Guku Africanus* and *J'accuse*, was telling: neither the judges nor the people seemed to know what would happen next. At first, it appeared as if people weren't willing to come up front to tell their stories. They must have been held by the spell of Mugabe's personality, it appeared. Or perhaps, Nkomo's booming voice confused them. It might be the combination of both.

As though to heighten the spell in the hall, or perhaps to give it an African calm, a warm contralto intoned a song that seamlessly filled into the silence. Many began to hum it. It was "Malaika," but the voice wasn't Makeba's. No, it was a much younger voice. Yvonne positioned her camera in search of the singer. It wasn't difficult to find her, for the voice had such clarity that it created a visible aura around the singer. Yvonne's jaw dropped as she peeped through her lens. "Thenjiwe," she whispered to herself, taking her eyes away from the lens so that they met with Thenjiwe's.

Mugabe, too, recognized Thenjiwe. He remembered that she was the decapitated one of the two sisters of Yvonne's story. Nonceba sat next to her sister. Yvonne returned her attention to her recording. The sound of a guitar rose from a corner beyond the hall to accompany the song, joined by five violins and two talking drums. The people gave up their humming and listened to the mellifluous song and the perfect synchrony of the instruments. They didn't mind that they came from elsewhere. And just as the song came to an end, a thin young man stood up and, stepping out of his pew, said at the top of his voice: "I have a story to tell. I have a story to tell!"

All eyes turned to him. Yvonne focused her camera on the young man as he walked to the fore and took the position Sontonga occupied earlier. Hurriedly, formally, he bowed to the throne, turned to the right and then to the left, to Mugabe, who raised his right hand to him in acknowledgment of his youthful wisdom.

"My name is Emerson Manyika," he said. "I don't know whether any person here knows me."

There was no reaction.

"My story is very simple," Emerson said.

"Tell us," some voices encouraged.

"My mother's family came to Zimbabwe from South Africa in the worst days of apartheid. They were three: my mother, uncles Steve and Luke. After two years in Zimbabwe, my uncles returned to South Africa where they fought alongside other antiapartheid heroes. My mother couldn't go back with them, for she was pregnant."

He glanced at the people and shrugged lightly; "Pregnant with me," he added. "So she married my father and became a Zimbabwean. I did not know her. She died two years after I was born. When I was a young boy growing up in Chegutu, my father took me to Harare. That was in 1986 and I was six years old.

"Harare was a very beautiful city. There were very good, asphalted roads, so smooth and clean that you could eat from any part. That was the first time I saw very tall houses. There were gardens with green lawns. There were flowerbeds everywhere. The sidewalks were well-kept and clean. Children played here and there: black children and white children. I was really proud of my country. My father said it was the best country in Africa, better than South Africa, better than Nigeria.

"My father was a teacher and he earned 200 Zimbabwean dollars a month. That was quite huge at the time. We had enough to eat, pay our rent, and save. He also sent about 10 dollars every month to my uncles to help them in their war against apartheid.

"So, when my father took me to Harare and gave me 50 cents to buy whatever I wanted, I didn't know what to do with that much money. It was exactly what we spent for bread, butter, and milk for about three days. At school, I spent just five cents a week for toffees and chewing gum. I couldn't spend all of the 50 cents."

He looked up. Some people were growing impatient. Just then a male voice rang out. "Is this the story of how you died?"

"Yes, I will come to that," he said. "Please, give me time. Okay, growing up, I wanted to become a soldier. I loved soldiers because they liberated. I wanted

12

to help build our nation. But my father told me that the best way to do that was to be a teacher. So, I became one. I began to teach eight years ago. I was proud that my father witnessed me becoming a teacher. I was also proud to show him my first paycheck, which was much more than he received. 5,000 Zim dollars.

"My father lived with me in Harare. I did not want him to live alone in Chegutu. He was not paid his pension. We had to make-do on my salary which, at the end of the month, did not always cover our expenses. But Mugabe understood the plight of the people and increased teacher salaries. It wasn't small at all. Just two years ago, I looked at my bank account. There were many zeroes behind the digit 2. I became a millionaire like many teachers. Well, like many people. We used plastic bags to carry money to the market. A loaf of bread cost 70,000 Zim dollars. For two liters of cooking oil I paid 100,000 Zim dollars.

"We did not understand what was going on in our country. Some radio stations said it was the plan of our former colonial masters that we should go down in pieces. The British people were behind our miseries. They sabotaged our economy. First, they gave us AIDS and now they made sure that we became poor. Things have gone bad. Veterans in ragged dress parade through the streets that are now potholed everywhere. Children no longer play in the gardens. Where once there were well-pruned flowerbeds, there are now high walls.

"Oh," he blurted and looked up to meet the eyes of the man who had expressed impatience with his tangential narrative, "I know that you all will think that I'm wasting your time because I tell what every Zimbabwean knows. I know that you all want to hear how I died. Well, to those who are impatient about the cause of my death, I would like to say that I was lynched. I died in South Africa."

"South Africa?" asked a female voice.

"Yes, in South Africa," Emerson went on.

"Then this is not a Zimbabwean story," another person said.

"It is a Zimbabwean story. I am a Zimbabwean. Just listen to me. You will understand. I don't want to leave out any important details of how I came to be lynched. So, please bear with me. I know that I am not a good storyteller, but I will come to the main point soon.

"Things continued to go bad, so bad that by the end of last year I lost my job. My father called my uncles and they told me to come to them. They would help me find a teaching job. So, I went."

He looked up and smiled faintly. "My uncles were very happy to welcome me," he went on. "They said that they would never forget how much my father helped them in their difficult times. They were also surprised that things were not going well in Zimbabwe. They swore that they knew Mugabe, whom they lovingly called Bob. Uncle Steve, the older of the two, said that Bob wasn't responsible for the downfall of Zimbabwe. Zimbabwe was falling apart because it was part of a European plan to keep Africa underdeveloped so that they could always rule Africa. Uncle Steve was a Marxist and believed that the new South African revolution was not yet complete. It would be complete the day the last white person left South Africa.

"Uncle Luke, on the other hand, said that no one else other than the leader should bear responsibility for what had gone wrong in a country. It was like in a family. If anything went wrong in a family, the head of the family bore responsibility. But he said that the world should try to understand Bob. Things started going bad in the country when his first wife, Sally, died."

Emerson stopped abruptly and glanced at Mugabe, who pursed his lips in an unmistakable pity-evoking posture. He shook his head.

"When Sally died," Emerson went on, "Bob began to lose his mind. Bob loved Sally more than anything. Sally loved Zimbabwe more than anything. So, while Sally was alive, things went well.

"My uncle reminded me that Bob was thrown into prison without being accused of anything. He did nothing. At Salisbury, where he was imprisoned, nine men shared a dark and dirty cell with too few beds and just one poop bucket. There, they were confined for 23 hours a day. Can you imagine that? Horrible! He received the sad news that his son, Nhamodzenyika, died in Ghana."

A collective sigh of empathy swept through the hall. It was, however, quickly replaced by some incomprehensible murmur that spoke of their confusion, a confusion emanating from an unfortunate blend of anger and empathy. It was empathy because people imagined themselves having the same experiences

14

Mugabe had while in prison; they imagined the hurt of being shouted down by white police, being ordered like a nonentity by Ian Smith. Yet, when they remembered what they had suffered at Mugabe's hands, their anger shot to the hall's ceiling. While they were tugged by these conflicting emotions, unsure where to rest their hearts, voices from outside penetrated the hall with stunning clarity: *The falcon cannot hear the falconer.*

Yvonne turned her camera to the bluish drape on the right. Truly, there were two men standing close to the drape, holding in their right hands what appeared to be glasses of wine. *Anarchy, mere anarchy*, one of the men said.

They adored him! the other said; *He came to them with thunder and lightning. They had never seen anything like it.*

The ceremony of innocence is drowned;
The best lack all convictions, while the worst
Are full of passionate intensity.

The other took a sip from his glass. *I, too, was afraid of him. He could have killed me.*

Emerson seemed troubled by the clear intrusion of these outside voices. No less was the audience. He looked around, and, shaking off the distraction, he raised his voice a bit to attract the attention of his listeners. "So, my story," he announced.

"Yes, your story, bro," said one young man. Emerson fixed his gaze at the young man as though he were the only person his story was meant for. "I didn't get the teaching job I hoped for in South Africa. Rather, I worked at a construction site," Emerson went on. "It was hard. I wasn't used to carrying heavy things like blocks and metals, but I was happy I had a job that paid me every month. I sent money to my father. There were many people from Zimbabwe, Mozambique, and Nigeria. Black South Africans did not like us. They accused us of taking their jobs away. They said we came to reap where we did not sow and that we should go back to where we came from. Some boasted that they would send us home by force. I did not know that it would mean that they would hunt us down like animals. I never believed that those who suffered like they did would go after others. But I was a fool. I deceived myself so much.

15

"Then came the day of my death. I was returning to work that day. I walked into an armed band of young black men at a roadblock. They had spears and machetes and tires and gallons of petrol. Some of them wore T-shirts on which war slogans were written. One read: *Freedom vigilante*. I thought they were young men out to check the rampant crime and rape in the black townships and neighborhoods. God, I was such a fool.

"I was a fool to have believed that those young men were out to do some good. No, they weren't. They were out to kill people. So, suddenly a mob burst out from behind me; I was trapped between the roadblock and the mob. They chanted something that sounded like war songs. Some from the mob appeared to recognize me. They shouted: 'He is from Zimbabwe. He is from Zimbabwe.' I knew that I was in a mess. There was no place to run.

"One of the men with machetes ran toward me, swinging his weapon. I wasn't quick enough. A blow fell on my forehead; I staggered back, and cried for help. But no help came. People looked away. Then another blow came from behind at the nape of my neck. I fell down. Then I felt the weight of a tire on my neck and the coldness of petrol all over my body. I felt the sudden biting hotness of the flames.

"That was it."

An elderly woman who sat in the second pew was wiping her tears. When her eyes met with Emerson's she sighed: "Oh, dear."

Emerson cleared his throat to hold back a surging torrent of emotion. "That was it," he repeated and went on to describe in detail his feelings at the time of his death. "A thick and dirty smoke soared to the sky as my body crackled in flames. A pillar of darkness. Some people were laughing. Some others were chanting South African songs. I was dying. Not long after the fire enveloped me, my spirit left my body."

He looked up.

"This is my story," he added, rounding off his narrative. "Robert Mugabe was there when I was born. He was there when I died."

Emerson turned to Mugabe and, making an obvious effort to overcome his reservations, blurted: "Why?"

Mugabe was not one to leave any challenge unanswered. As soon as he noticed Emerson's sudden change of tone, he sprang to his feet so that every person turned toward him. "You have been misled," he shouted. "You were brainwashed in South Africa! They fed you their racist propaganda."

Ghostly voices echoed his words from behind him in a practiced uniformity: *Racist propaganda! Racist propaganda.* People looked around, not knowing from where exactly the voices came. Mugabe, unfazed by the voices, went on with his defense. "White racist apartheid propaganda," he said again.

White racist apartheid propaganda echoed the same voices back to him.

"So, you doubt that Emerson was attacked?" asked Equiano.

"Racism," Mugabe said. "He was listening to BBC."

As though to arrest the obvious monotony of the repetition, another voice from the same corner raised a question: *What have you learned from the European man?* It was then that Mugabe showed some irritation with the nagging voices. He looked around fiercely and, face contorted, shot back: "Can anything good come from the European man?"

It was as if he talked to the wind.

Emerson raised his hand to the chief judge in a gesture that pleaded for attention. Equiano responded. "Yes, anything to add to your story?" he asked.

"Nothing, sir. I just want to tell you that it is on YouTube."

"Emerson's death is on YouTube," Equiano told Mugabe.

"YouTube?" Mugabe asked. "The instrument of white magic propaganda?"

The three judges looked at one another, rather surprised by Mugabe's words, blurted without much thought. Equiano turned to Yvonne and asked her whether it could be found on YouTube. She stepped back to her pew and retrieved a small keyboard, typed into it and looked up. A white screen rolled down just in front of the judges.

As the title "Flames of Hate" flashed, people murmured in disapproval of what was surely to come. They were nervous, certain that they would see the ugliness of the Africa they knew, the image of Africa they all were eager to see eliminated by this trial.

Is *Guku* essentially African? For God's sake, it is not. Just as love is a universal feeling, so is *Guku*. *Guku* is an expression of a people's collective denial of all life instinct, a death wish for which the dictator is merely a ready executioner.

Guku is the clichéd art of believing that one's problems exist in the other and that the way to solve those problems is to eliminate the other.

Guku is a vicious expression of the long-repressed need to avenge oneself for a perceived wrong. It usually arises out of a strong, if delusional, feeling of moral excellence attributable to being a victim.

Guku is borne of the spirit of *ressentiment*, in which case a person develops a *gukunized* personality. The logic of a *gukunized* personality runs thus: I am a victim, therefore I cannot be blamed for any wrong, therefore I am right. A *gukunized* mindset finds nothing wrong in killing or harming other people because he already justifies this on the grounds of his having been harmed earlier.

The Sad Story of Erica Maidai as Told by Herself

Emerson's question, that one-word interrogative interjection, *why*, quickly drained all life from Mugabe's face. Conversely, it restored some appreciative smiles to Yvonne's. Her chest heaved with excitement: for her, the trial had finally taken off. Having followed Emerson with her camera until he returned to his pew, she stepped back and adjusted it to capture the members of the audience, some of whom were wiping their tears while others merely stared ahead, visibly numbed by the reality of the YouTube video they had watched. As though following Emerson's cue, a woman's voice rang out from the last pew on the left: "I, too, have a question for Robert Mugabe."

People turned in her direction. A somewhat stocky, light-skinned black woman with high cheekbones and prominent breasts she appeared to be proud of, for she walked chest-up. She exuded absolute self-confidence that commanded their immediate attention. She had big, almond-shaped, soft eyes over a short, proudly broad nose that added flashes of beauty to her oval face. She could have been in her early or mid forties. She walked to the front and took the position vacated by Emerson. Turning to the people, she repeated what she had said from her pew. "I have many questions for Robert Mugabe!" But her statement, rather than command as much attention as her physique did, rattled the people who were obviously more eager to listen to stories. "No, no," a man's voice rang out. "We have no time for more questions. We are here to tell stories."

"Stories do not exclude questions," the woman answered, looking at him more challengingly.

"But the chief judge said we're here for stories," another man's voice chimed. "Just stories, you understand. No more questions, please."

Quickly realizing that it was unwise to risk losing the attention of the many thousands of ears, she eased the muscles of her face, and smiled faintly. "My question is only a preamble to my story," she said pleadingly.

Her otherwise shy smile boldly widened on her attractive face. It had its desired effect. Some people smiled back and some men breathed out rather softly, succumbing to her feminine charisma; even the chief judge was moved by the sudden change in the young woman's tone. "Okay, ask your question," he intervened. "But do it quickly. We are running out of time."

"Thank you very much, your lordship. But I think we have no duties to attend to," she said looking around, still smiling. "This is African Afterlife, isn't it?"

"Sure it is," echoed some voices.

Equiano was thrilled by the woman's audacity. There was little doubt that she knew what she was saying and would tell a gripping story that would reveal a lot about Mugabe. Happy for the answer she elicited, she turned to Robert Mugabe, whose gaze was directed toward the throne as if he were waiting for God to intervene in what was obviously becoming a scheme to bring him down. "I ask you, Your Majesty," the woman said aloud so that Mugabe jerked and then looked at her, face contorted in a sneer. "I ask you: What are Zimbabweans to you?"

"How can you ask me that stupid question?" Mugabe shouted. He turned to the judges. "I have not come here to be quizzed by a woman."

"Sit down," Equiano ordered. "This is not Zimbabwe."

Mugabe looked around nervously. His eyes rested for a while on Joshua Nkomo who was sharing some chuckle with Muzorewa. Some people also laughed. Visibly relishing the unsettling effect of her question on him, she repeated it, this time turning to the audience as though to make sure that they understood the implication of that one question. The people's silence appeared to have fed her will. Nkomo and Muzorewa conferred, at the same time flashing admiring glances at the woman. Seeing these eminent men encourage her with their smiles made her realize the enormous import of her position. She became self-conscious. Was she capable of rendering her story in a way that would satisfy them? Did she really understand the magnitude of her own question? The stage fright which she had not experienced before took hold of her. She froze. Then, another voice, a friendly one, called, "Go on, dear sister." It was Nkomo. "Tell us your story," he said.

"Tell us your story!" many voices echoed.

Coming back to herself, she thanked them for making her feel at home in their presence. "I will tell you how I died," she said. "I begin by saying that, unlike Emerson, I did not die in the slums of South Africa. I died in Zimbabwe—in my homeland, right in the heart of Mashonaland. I, too, am a child of *Chimurenga*."

"You are not!" shouted Mugabe. "You must be a traitor."

"This man must be mad," a voice yelled.

"Quiet please," the chief judge said, knocking his gavel on the table for attention. He then turned to Mugabe. "Sir, we respect your right to free speech. You must also respect order and decency in this court."

He turned to his fellow judges. They nodded in accord. It was then that Marechera turned to Mugabe. "Sir, we all are children of *Chimurenga*," he said. "We fought the occupation of our land. We fought oppression. Every one of us did. So, you are wrong to deny the woman's participation in our common struggle."

After upbraiding Mugabe, Marechera gave the woman a sign to continue with her story. She made a slight bow in the direction of the judges and, turning to the people, introduced herself. "My name is Erica Maidai. I was born in 1962, 18 years before Zimbabwean independence. I graduated with honors from the education department of the University of Zimbabwe. Until my death, I taught at Ngezi Secondary School. I was married. I had two sons. One of them died shortly after birth. The other lives with my mother. My husband died of tuberculosis. He, too, was a teacher. I know that you might be wondering why I am telling all this. It is neither to attract pity nor to prove that I am better than anybody. Indeed, I am no better. No, I just wanted to let you understand where I am coming from. I was 46 years old when I died. Just beginning to live, you might say. Or perhaps already old enough to die. Old enough, perhaps, according to Zimbabwean life expectancy.

"But I am also old enough to claim as much honor and self-respect as Zimbabwe does. Old enough to tell our story. I might not be as wise as some of you," she swept her right hand in the direction of the audience, then toward the judges and Nkomo and his group. "I might not be as gifted as our writers," she said as her eyes met with Yvonne's. "No, I might not, but I am wise enough to know that we Africans have deceived ourselves for a much longer time."

"Yes, tell us, sister," a voice rang.

"She talks like white people," Mugabe yelled. "She condemns us Africans. Didn't you hear it? She blames us. A traitor!"

"It is now time for me to talk to this mad man," Nkomo said, springing to his feet.

Biko stood up and extended his hands to the left and to the right. "Hold your rage!" he ordered, and turning to Nkomo. "You, too, have many questions to answer, sir."

The shock on Nkomo's face was unmistakable. He quietly sat back. Biko motioned to Erica to go on with her story.

"Thank you very much," Erica said. "I was saying that we Zimbabweans have deceived ourselves long enough. We have been turning and turning around us in an ever-shrinking gyre. The circle never widens. Our horizons never broaden. We have our heads in sand, and claws out to the world, believing it will keep us safe."

"Good poem," a voice said, initiating a measure of applause.

Erica nodded in admission and went on with her story: "I know what it means to be colonized. It is no different than being a slave. Your condition is always a nervous condition."

"Yes, nervous condition," another voice repeated.

Erica allowed a faint smile and went on. "Because of my age and standing, I appreciate what Zimbabwe felt like under Ian Smith. I know what it meant to go to a white school and be insulted by white boys and girls who weren't half as good as you were. I know what it meant to be called a *kaffir* to your face by a white boy and your principal, a white nun, laughed. I know what it meant to be excluded from the school's O level roll of honor even though you were the best in your class. All because you're black."

She was impressed by the rapt attention the people paid to her while she enumerated some of the humiliating experiences that many of them obviously shared.

"It is with the weight of history that I speak. I speak because one of our writers taught us that it is immoral not to raise your voice when it is needed. That was Alexander Kanengoni. He said that lies begin the very moment we keep silent about things that really matter. Silence spills into everyday lives of our people

22

and translates itself into fear. A people who live in fear is a dead people. I swore not to give in to silence; I swore not to live in fear."

Yvonne took up her paper and pen and made notes.

"I thought that my honor lay in the fact that I should not compromise my opinions. My choices. My decisions. That, I thought, was the principle upon which Mbuya Nehanda, our ancestress, fought the white man. It was the principle upon which our veterans fought many endless wars. They gave their lives to grant us black folks the right to a decent life and to freedom. It is only in the abundance of freedom that we can be held accountable for our actions. That was the principle that justified the being of Zimbabwe. Life. Liberty. A decent life. Those were exactly what led me, after years of tough mental wrangling, to renounce my support of Robert Mugabe and to join the Movement for Democratic Change. My MDC party membership was based on the simple truth that opposition without grassroots activism was useless. Following the words of Mahatma Ghandi, I wanted to become the change I desired. It was as an activist for freedom and for a better life that I died. I died fighting for freedom."

A sigh of empathy went through the audience.

"You died as an agent of white racists," murmured Mugabe; some people snickered.

That did not disturb Erica as she appeared now to have taken full grip of her narrative. She went on: "Mugabe lost my total sympathy on his 20th anniversary as Zimbabwean prime minister. That was when he proposed a constitutional amendment to expand his presidential power. Power corrupts and 20 years in power corrupts 20 times over. The first to get the taste of his Machiavellian flavor of power were the white people who did not flee Zimbabwe. Thousands of veterans seized white-owned farms. This much we all know.

"It was exactly after the invasion of white farms that I realized that Mugabe had not only overstayed his heroism, he had also gone crazy, mad."

"Who has gone crazy?" Mugabe asked, springing to his feet.

The soldier sitting by his right tried to rein him in, "Your excellency," he whispered, tapping him gently on his arm.

"Don't hold me back," he roared. "Didn't you hear what she said about me?

That I am mad. Do I look like a mad man?" He then turned to Erica. "It is you who has gone crazy. You have betrayed your fatherland. You are not a true woman."

People began to laugh loudly as it gradually became evident to them that one person in the hall was indeed mentally impaired.

"Quiet, please," the chief judge commanded and then turned to Mugabe. "Sit down," he said.

"So, as I was saying," Erica went on, "I knew that we were headed for ruin. Our beloved country, our dear beautiful Zimbabwe. I knew I had to do something. But I must confess that I didn't join the opposition right away. I was afraid of the consequences. I thought I shouldn't endanger my life. But it was surely raw cowardice, laziness. Well, I had to be shaken from my slumber one day. It was on Wednesday, March 13, 2002, to be exact. That day, following the election that should have been won by the opposition leader, Morgan Tsvangirai, Mugabe declared himself the winner."

She shrugged glumly. "You would say that I am naïve to have believed that only those who deserved to lose elections actually lose. I should have known that power concedes nothing without a demand, as the American Frederick Douglass once said. Power is never handed over on a platter of gold. So, how could Mugabe have lost if people didn't actively seek his loss, if people didn't form a strong opposition? Could he lose if we all sat back and thought that things would happen by merely wishing for them to happen?

"Two years later, I joined the opposition in Mashonaland West. People laughed at us. We were so stupid to think that we could win any seat in Mugabe's home province. The decision wasn't easy, but it was inevitable. This is how it all began: One day, I read about the upcoming rally for political awareness in the Alternative Mashonaland community newsletter called *The Village Conscience*."

"Oh, *The Village Conscience*," shouted a young man. "I read it, too."

Erica nodded. "It was good."

"Yes, it was," said the young man.

"The announcement called for people with conscience, old and young, to come out and raise their voices against the decay and entrenched corruption in the land. It announced that our country was about to fall apart."

"Things have fallen apart," sighed a light-skinned elderly black man, scratching his bald head.

"Yes, things fall apart," echoed another voice a few pews behind him.

Erica smiled. "Yes, indeed. The newsletter said that the Mugabe regime failed to deliver the promises of independence. Rather it enslaved the populace in a way that is no longer different from the style of the British colonial masters. This is what the newsletter said: whoever supported the war against colonial masters should ask himself what he really fought for—not only what he fought against. It was this difference: fighting for and fighting against that caught my attention. When I realized the great difference, I, too, began to be aware of what I fought for. What I fought for was eternal; it has value. I realized that the real *chimurenga*, the *chimurenga* of everyday life consisted not in seeing the demise of the other, but in taking control of your life, in living and living fully.

"I was pleased to find that Tapiwa Mugwandarikwa, the secretary of the Mashonaland West wing of the opposition party, signed the newsletter. Tapiwa was my old secondary school teacher and one of those who shaped my life. He was a small, but sturdy man, with a rugged face that reminded one of Morgan Tsvangirai—fierce but determined. It was he who awakened my interest in Alexander Kanengoni, whose *Echoing Silences* he made us read. Tapiwa invited me to a pre-rally gathering at St. Fidelis' Catholic Church in Mabvuku. I became one of his assistants.

"So, we took off. I became a political animal. Well, I soon had the typical experience of political animals. In 2005, our party lost the March parliamentary election to the ruling Zanu-PF. However, rather than discourage us, the loss fueled our activism. We knew it wasn't a free and fair election, but we had no means to challenge the result. We started working toward the next election. When we asked the elderly to compare how they felt then with how they felt during the Ian Smith regime, they said that there was no difference. Some even said that life under Ian Smith was far better. They even wished for him to return. Oh, well, that wasn't what we wanted to hear. Nevertheless, we assured them that we would make a difference. They should give us a chance. Luckily, we were convincing people at the rate we hadn't hoped for.

25

"But it hadn't been an easy time for me. I had a series of personal and family misfortunes. On Saturday, March 11, 2007, I gave birth to my second child who did not survive. That was not going to be the only bad news for me that weekend. The following day, it was reported that Morgan Tsvangirai has been attacked by armed men suspected to be war veterans. They had cornered him while he was attending a banned protest rally. Just as I was recovering from child delivery and the child's death, John, my husband, who had been suffering from tuberculosis, succumbed to the illness."

A barrage of sighs rolled through the hall. But Erica went straight on without allowing the mellow feelings to dull her narrative edge. "John made his passing much easier, though. Before his death he told me that he was proud to know me. He said that he was going to God and he would watch over me and our son, John Jr. He encouraged me not to give up the fight because that meant a lot to the future of our son. Somehow, I felt he was always with me. I fought on, happy to have had a man in my life who shared the same values with me. I went to meetings, rallies, and demonstrations against rising inflation and against the government. I should have known that the road to freedom was steeper than I could ever have imagined. I should have known that more suffering and humiliation awaited me.

"They weren't long in coming. In the second week of June, just about five weeks following my husband's death, I received an anonymous letter detailing my movement and activities in the recent past. It described with precision what I had done and sketches of what I had said in most gatherings. The letter stated that I was betraying the blood of those who died for our independence by supporting Tsvangirai. I was asked to not only stop attending those rallies but also to renounce my membership of the opposition party openly. God, I was frightened; I knew that I was already in their net. However, I went on with my activism. I, too, am a child of *Chimurenga*. I, too, was touched by the spirit of Mbuya Nehanda.

"And just as Nehanda was not intimidated by white people's threats, I did not allow Mugabe's veterans to silence me. Toward the end of July, I received a batch of male visitors, whose visit was intended as a warning of worse things to come. It was late in the night. I was getting ready to retire. Just then I heard

26

a vehicle in front of my house. Seconds later, furious bangs sounded on my door. My heart fell into my stomach. I felt dizzy, knowing that it must be the veterans. I dashed into John's room. He was sleeping. I thought of waking him up and telling him to hide, but I quickly buried the idea, knowing it was already too late. I opened the door. I had hardly done so when an armed, masked man forcefully pulled me out of the house. He pointed a pistol to my head and murmured: *make any noise and you're dead*. I did not make any noise.

"He motioned that I should move toward their vehicle which had its headlights on. I couldn't see what was behind it. The masked man was still pointing his gun at my head and nudging me with his left hand. He smelled of Chibuku beer and hashish. I held my left hand in front of my face to fend off the abrasive light. In the midst of the dread that had taken hold of me, I heard John's voice. 'Mama, Mama,' he called. 'Mama, where are you going?'

"'Go back to bed,' I told to him. 'I'll be coming back soon.'

"I prayed that he wouldn't run after me. Thank God, he did not. Two men were waiting for us. One was by the driver's door while the other was inside. My kidnapper pushed me inside where the other dragged me in with an unsurprising greeting. 'Traitor!'

"The one who said it went on to force my hands behind my back where he tied them with a tiny rope. He, too, smelled.

"'You got our letter, didn't you?' the other asked.

"'Which letter?'

"'So, you didn't get our warning?' the one who tied my hands asked. The voice sounded somehow familiar, but I couldn't place it. I said nothing. 'Answer me!' he shouted, nudging me hard.

"The other tried to calm him. 'It's okay,' he said. 'We shall teach her.'

"And saying that, he reached for my face, did a mock caressing and quickly slid down to my breasts and pressed. 'Still good. She's still fresh,' he said to his colleague,. The other went on toying with my breasts, his breath getting louder in ways that made his desire apparent.

"We did not drive very far. Just about three kilometers from the village. They stopped at an open space, near a crossroad and ordered me to get out of the vehicle, which I did, shivering. As soon as I stepped down, they dragged me to the front of the vehicle. They ripped apart my top so that my breasts showed, then rent my skirt and my underwear.

"I didn't want to beg them. It would be useless. Nor would any attempt to run into the nearby bush be helpful. I did whatever they told me to do and prayed that raping me would be the least of the harms they would inflict on me. I was thinking about Junior. Somebody had to be there for him. It was helpful that my mind was on him while the men defiled me. The last one to get off of me uttered in a gruff, grating voice intended to etch the assault deeper in my soul: 'Next time you know not to betray your people.'

"I was finally able to match the voice with a face. It was that of Mayoyo, one of the veterans who boasted openly that Zimbabwe belonged to them and they could take whatever they wanted.

"I lay on the ground for a while, at first not believing they had gone, not believing that I was alive. But I was. Pain reminded me that I was. There was pain in my heart. And in the pit of my stomach. There was pain between my legs. I swear they used iron rods. The pain burned through my spine and up to my head. The pervasive acrid odor of alcohol and hashish was no less offensive. I scuttled up.

"All around me was darkness. Discordant noises emerged from the nearby bushes. Like a blind person, I groped around for my clothes. I hugged what remained of my cloths to my chest and my groin and began to trace my way back home. I shook my head vigorously to force back a wave of tears on the brink of surging forth. Then I murmured some words of encouragement to myself. No tears. No tears. I shouldn't allow what had just been done to me to destroy me spiritually. No, those men weren't strong enough to kill my morale. *Fear not he who could kill the body, fear he who could kill your soul.*

"I staggered inside the house. John was frightened to death. He had cried himself into a shivering mass, hiding in a corner of our sitting room. I told him I was sorry for leaving and consoled him the best I could. I then walked straight into my bathroom for a bath. I scrubbed, scrubbed, and scrubbed off everything that I could think of. I scrubbed where their bodies contacted mine. The stench of their breath, what they poured inside me.

"At the same time, I was sadly aware that there was something I couldn't

28

wash off. My heart came to a stop the moment I thought about that. I couldn't wash it off. To be raped by a veteran was to become infected with a VD, veteran disease. Recently, members of the war veterans have been dying in twos and threes weekly. They were those who raped women indiscriminately during their reign of terror in the past decade. They boasted that AIDS was a white man's disease and had no power over the black man, much less a war veteran. I was sure I had been infected.

"The next morning, I promised Junior I would never leave him again. Yet three days later, I took him to my mother, also a widow. I explained to her what happened to me. Her reaction was not far from what I expected. 'You have to stop going to those meetings,' she advised.

"'No, Mama. I won't stop. You know I can't stop.'

"'But you can't change the world alone.'

"'Yes, Mama, but I can't change myself.'

"'They will come after you again,' she said, defeated.

"I knew that the veterans would come for me again. They would demand that I become a member of Zanu-PF. If it was my life they wanted, they could have easily gotten rid of me. I knew it would be a huge gain for them if I renounced my membership in the opposition party. They would celebrate it as much as they celebrated the conversion of Professor Jonathan Moyo, who used to be a fierce critic of Robert Mugabe, but who became an equally fierce supporter of the prime minister's repressive policies. No, they wouldn't get me. I went into hiding; I spent nights at different places.

"Many of our members also went into hiding. They no longer spent nights in their houses. I hoped we wouldn't have to live like that for long because the next election wasn't far off. That would be in March 2008. My hopes were not dashed. Our party snatched five seats in Mashonaland West. So we thought we had sealed Mugabe's defeat.

"But we were in for a rude awakening. He announced that God put him in office and that only God could therefore remove him. He consequently swore to fight the result. That infuriated us all. How on earth could he claim that God ordained him the perpetual lord over us all? I was so mad with his utterance that I swore that not even the devil could stop me from working for the opposition.

"I shouldn't have called the devil's name, for as soon as I did, he responded. He came to me. The first sign of his coming was on April 13, when Tapiwa Mugwandarikwa was stabbed to death while returning from a Sunday service. The news upset me more than the pain of my rape by the veterans. I felt I was the person who had been stabbed. I knew I could be the next to die, but I wasn't ready to quit. Quitting would only grant Mugabe unbridled power over the populace.

"So, daring the devil, I attended his funeral the following day. The devil came. He met me on my way back from the funeral. I was in a group of two women and two young men. Suddenly a Toyota HIACE delivery van pulled up in front of us. Three armed, masked men jumped out of the vehicle and one of them fired into the air. We all dove to the ground and began to scramble to safety. But we didn't get far. Two of the men dashed for me. They caught me and pulled me up from the ground. One of them punched me in my stomach. The pain was so intense I could hardly breathe.

"They dragged me into the vehicle where two other men were waiting and drove off. The men inside the van weren't masked. I knew them. One of them welcomed me in the same gruff voice that had warned me the day I was raped. He was the last man to get off me. Mayoyo. The other man had his back to the door, so I couldn't see his face. Mayoyo reached for a white piece of cloth that looked like a headscarf and blindfolded me while the other tied my hands behind me. I didn't offer any resistance."

Erica looked up at the people. They were so rapt she thought they were indeed dreaming with eyes wide open. Then she glanced at Mugabe. He was staring at a point in front of him; he did not look up. She turned to the listeners. "I am nearing the end of my story. I am sorry that it has taken me so long to tell."

"Oh, no, no, go on please," some voices said in a loud chorus. "Go on. We are with you, sister."

She nodded in gratitude, noticing at the same time that some people looked as though they were about to cry. She didn't want any tears; she didn't want any pity. So, she forced a smile to underscore her mastery of the situation and went on: "I started my long story by asking a simple question. I asked, 'What are Zimbabweans to Mugabe?'"

She cleared her throat to regain her voice, which cracked with emotion at the question. "This was the only question that kept echoing in my mind when those men kidnapped me. I lay flat on the floor of the van, knowing that I had come to the end of my life. The two masked men, I could guess, sat in the front while Mayoyo and the second man sat on the floor, each partly resting their feet on my torso. They said nothing. The van screeched and moaned as it danced its way through the bumpy, potholed roads of our town. My heart was racing in my chest like a hamster in a spinning wheel. My mind ran to every angle of the world and to nowhere in particular. I tried to will my mind out of that van and think not of me, nor of John Jr. I tried not to think of the future. There was none. There was only night.

"I followed the noise of the engine, imagining where they were taking me. I could feel that the van had left the asphalt and was now on dirt roads when it began to sway more; we were no longer just running into shallow potholes, but literally diving into ditches and crawling out of them. The gears screeched loudly every time the driver shifted. Sure, they were taking me to where they would dump my body. God, let them not make me suffer terrible pain. Let it be quick.

"After a while, one of the men turned on the radio as I could infer from the clicking sound of a pressed button. A song began to play. It was Thomas Mapfumo, 'Musha Wenyu (Your Home).' I could no longer hold back my tears as I listened to the lyrics and thought about my home. Was it still my home? Could I be proud of my identity as a Zimbabwean? What was there to be proud of? Independence? What is independence without human freedom? What is independence without decency of life? Our people did not fight for a new form of slavery. They did not fight for poverty and disease. They fought to eradicate them. Suddenly, tears swelled my eyes.

"I wished for nothing than to have the blindfold removed so that my tears could flow freely. I wanted to cry for my beautiful Zimbabwe that was no longer beautiful. It had become the home of war veterans.

"A few more songs from his album, *Toi Toi (Protest),* played before it was shut down. Shortly after, the engine also was turned off. We were at our destination. I hadn't the faintest idea where we were, nor did I care to know.

31

As far as I was concerned, the song was my requiem.

"When they opened the door, a chant by a chorus of young voices surged in. I was at first pleased that they hadn't taken me to the remotest part of the jungle where they would dump my body. I was happy to be among other people. And they were singing! From another corner came another group of voices. They weren't singing. They were repeating in unison the words that a more mature voice issued in a commanding tone: 'To hell with white Satan.'

"*'To hell with white Satan.'*

"'Never again shall we be slaves of whites!'

"*'Never again shall we be slaves of whites.'*

"'Never again British rule!'

"*'Never again British rule!'*

"I could hear a mix of male and female voices. Their feet stomped the earth in a somewhat regular pattern. My captors dragged me out of the van; one of the men ripped the piece of cloth off my face. I was so blinded by the sudden rush of light that I had to close my eyes for a while. I gradually opened them and found myself standing in a large open area. I looked around. At my distant left, I saw a large, brown board attached to a two-meter-long peg. On the board was written in scraggly writing: 'Black Power Farm.' Two long I-shaped buildings stood in my view. They looked like abandoned school buildings. There weren't just two groups of youths singing or receiving commands. There were many other groups scattered here and there. Some of them sang, while some did pushups.

"Three boys knelt under a big acacia in front of one of the buildings. They had their hands raised while three other slightly older boys flogged them. I was left standing while the van drove away. About 20 meters away from the buildings was another structure, a townhouse. I didn't need to guess where I had arrived. I had heard of it a number of times. I never doubted that such camps existed. But I never thought I would eventually be in the net of Mugabe's Green Bombers.

"They were proudly designated as Zimbabwe's domestic Peace Corps. I stood still where I had alighted from the van wondering what would happen to me next. It didn't take long to find out. Two young men in their early twenties led me away. Behind one of the two buildings, about two dozen men and women of different ages sat under a thatched shade with conical roof. Some had swollen lips, bandaged eyes, and sore arms.

"A man in a tattered military uniform addressed them. I was brought to him. At first, he appeared to ignore me and went on to address the group, telling them about the necessity of the third *chimurenga*. Gradually, though, he turned his head in my direction without moving his shoulders. His eyes were nearly as red as clumps of fresh blood. He called my name in a slow, ceremonial way. I answered. In the same way, he withdrew his gaze, facing the group as though he was to address them. He did not address them. He orchestrated a solemn silence, staring at some point in the floor in front of him. Just like a village witch doctor. 'Why have you betrayed us?' he asked as if talking to himself.

I didn't know how to answer that question.

"'I am asking you, Erica. Why have you become a white people's spy?'

"'I am not a spy,' I said.

"He turned fully to me and bellowed. 'You are! You have allowed yourself to be used. British colonial masters have used you!'

"'The British colonial masters did not use me,' I answered in the same measured tone I had used earlier.

"Returning to his earlier witch doctor-solemn pose, he asked, 'Why have you forgotten that you are a woman?'

"I did not answer—not even after he repeated his question. A few women in the group nodded to me, blinking their eyes, in what I interpreted to be urgings for me to cooperate. But I didn't know how to cooperate."

Erica took a deep breath and then went on in a pity-evoking tone. "Like you all, I loved my fatherland. I had no other place than that. I only wanted to live like regular human beings everywhere. But when I was brought to the camp I knew Zimbabwe had no place for me. Nor did it have any place for the men and women I met there. I was attracted to and appalled by the bloated lips, swollen eyes, and bandaged arms of these men and women. God, what did they do to be treated this way? Was this the price they paid for being Zimbabweans?

"I was still transfixed by the enormity of the suffering on their faces when the man in a tattered military uniform nodded to the two young men standing beside me. Following his orders, they ripped off my blouse and my bra. He stepped forward, fixing his bloodshot eyes on me. Even from afar, one could smell alcohol on his breath. He came closer, looked me straight in the eye, and then almost ceremoniously reached for my left breast. He pinched and twisted my nipple as one would a hard fruit to force out its seed. A sharp arrow darted up to my brain and initiated a bout of dizziness.

"In the same manner, he reached for the right one and did the same. The pain spread to every part of my body like many fingers of lightning striking the earth. My knees wobbled and I had to keep myself from crumbling. Topping the pain was shame. It's one thing to be raped by men whom you thought were beastly. But it's another thing entirely to stand naked in front of other men and women while a strange man toyed with your parts. This last bit prodded my tears; I closed my eyes and let my tears free flow. He chuckled mockingly. 'She cries like a girl,' he said and suddenly ground his teeth, his face contorted.

"He turned to the two young men. 'It's your turn,' he said and as though nothing happened, returned his gaze to the group he had been addressing. The two young men didn't need to hear the order again. One of them walked behind the thatched hut and returned with a thin, one-meter-long cable that looked like a computer mouse cord. The other held me steady while he used the cord on me—on my bare breasts! Whichever way I quickly turned, the whip found a new way to either of my breasts. I could do no more than groan like a child.

"The two young men led me past a group of girls who were being drilled to a marching parade, into one of the I-shaped houses. The building had different divisions of large sleeping cubicles. They pushed me into a room that was separated from another by a thin cardboard wall. Three mats lay spread on the floor. A young woman, about 16 years old, sat on one of them, curled in a fetal position. She was rocking to and fro, her face dug between her knees that were held by her two hands crossed just below the knees.

"I was still standing there, nursing the stinging pain in my breasts, when three men came in. One of them walked straight to the girl, unbuttoned his trousers, and instantly pulled them off. She did not resist. Face against the wall, she parted her legs. One of the other two unbuttoned his trousers, pulled them off and stepped closer to me.

34

"I did not react, did not even look up at him. I was overwhelmed by nausea and revulsion. For the first time in my life I thought of killing a human being. As though in response to my thought, he swung his right hand, striking a heavy blow on my head. I crumbled to the floor. I was faintly aware that somebody fumbled with my underwear and that something began to happen between my legs.

"I woke up half-way, with the man's weight fully on me. I felt pain everywhere. My thighs still spread, the second man came in. When they were done, two other men came for their turn. They were younger than the other two, about 20 or so. One of them went to the girl, the other came to me. By the time the sixth man arrived, I was inured to the pain between my legs. It appeared to have switched itself off. After him, a rag-wearing man in his mid-fifties came in. He did not demand that I keep my thighs open for him. He stood still, looking at me as if I were scum. 'Welcome to *pungwe*,' he said grumpily. 'All around the bush are our boys. You cannot escape.'

"For the night, five other women were shoved into our room so that the seven of us shared the three mats.

"The following morning, we were taken for a round of marching exercise after which, together with 20 others, mostly adults, we were taken to the thatched shade for re-education. On empty stomachs. The re-education took a predictable course of rehashing the history of Zimbabwe and the glories of its wars of liberation. The British were trying to take over our land through Morgan Tsvangirai, and through globalization. Who were we, then, to raise our voices against Mugabe who sacrificed everything for us? There was no doubt that we had all been guilty of supporting the MDC. We could redeem ourselves if we renounced our support of the party that had been proven to work only in the interest of white people.

"The man sitting beside me had a swollen eye and a heavy bulge on his left temple. Other men seemed to have received lesser beatings because not many bruises could be seen on their faces. Nearly all the women kept their eyes down, as if they had lost something in an imaginary crack of the earth.

"After the speech, we were told to recant our support of Tsvangirai—in the words that were spoken by one of the veterans. 'We recognize that Zanu-PF is the party of *Chimurenga*. We recognize that Robert Mugabe is our hero. We recognize that the opposition is the instrument of white colonial masters. We renounce every aspect of MDC.'

"Three of us did not repeat those words. Two men and I. I had the vague feeling that the men were Ndebele. Perhaps they were dissidents. I couldn't be sure since I didn't exchange words with them. Just a hunch based entirely on their looks. One of the men was dragged in front of us and, after venting his rage at him, the commander pulled his pistol, pointed it at the man's head, turned back at us as though to make sure we were looking, and, turning back to the man, pulled the trigger. The man slumped to the ground like a bag of corn. The veteran turned to the second man and, pointing his pistol to his head, asked him whether he was ready to renounce his support of the opposition. The second man, teeth chattering, hands shivering feverishly, renounced. Yet the commander's finger did not leave the trigger. A shot rang.

"It was now my turn. He asked me whether I was ready to renounce my allegiance to the opposition party. I said no. I didn't believe it would make any difference whether I renounced or not. He gnashed his teeth. Luckily for me, his finger had left the trigger. He took a deep breath and, in a fit of anger, hit my left temple with the gun and ordered me back to my cubicle.

"I was left there to nurse my pain. I purposely left the blood that dripped from the wound running. No, I didn't want to wipe it. Oddly enough, I took pride in my wound. After a while, the veteran walked into that room with two teenage boys. On seeing me soaked in my blood, he told one of the boys to go get a cloth; the blood was wiped off me. He ordered them to strip me and they did. He asked one of them to mount me at the same time thundering his order that I should spread my legs, which I did. The two boys had their turns. Poor boys, I thought. Did they know they had just had their death sentence handed to them? Or were they already tainted?

"I wasn't raped for the next two days, nor was I beaten. Rather, I was made to listen to series of Mugabe speeches with a few other people. Listening to those speeches was no less torturous to me either. They were nearly the same, merely variations on the same historical themes of colonialism, white supremacy, and our duty to reject them. Almost every one of them began with

36

the rhetorical question "What is Zimbabwe to Britain?" I recalled that the question was the centerpiece of his 2007 UN address, which was carried live over national radio. We knew his answers to this question: to Britain, Zimbabwe was merely an outpost. To Britain, Zimbabwe was a backyard of global concerns. To Britain, Zimbabwe was a place for cheap mineral resources. To Britain, Zimbabwe was a place a white man could kill thousands of blacks and go free.

"It was a nightmare listening to his address—even more so when one of the veterans gave us extra lectures on the hidden meaning of the speeches and what more we needed to know about Zimbabwe. Mugabe has been called a dictator because he stood up to the supremacist view of colonialists and stood in the way of whites who believed that blacks must be perpetually slaves of the world.

"In a private session with one of the commanders, I was asked whether I could challenge any of these things associated with Mugabe and I shook my head. 'No, they were true,' I said. 'Mugabe is our hero.'

"'Why, then, are you against him?' the interrogator asked.

"'I am for a better person,' I answered.

"'For a stooge of the West?'

"'No, Tsvangirai is not a stooge.'

"'Why then does the West support him?'

"'Why do majority of Zimbabweans support him?' I asked.

"'They are brainwashed.'

"'People are dying. Many others are fleeing to other countries. Our country is falling apart.'

"'So you call our liberation sacrifices suffering?'

"I said nothing. Nor did I respond to his other words aimed at making me realize my folly. After a while, he stopped, looked down at me, and left as though believing that I would soon come to believe the goal of Zimbabwean salvation.

"For the fourth straight night, I was neither raped nor beaten. I thought it was a grace time, time for me to rethink my position. Weirdly enough, some part of my mind clung to the single idea that Mugabe sacrificed his life for us all. Could it be that I was being an ingrate? This idea went through my mind like a merry-go-round and I could hardly pay attention to any other thing happening around me; the cries of many young women and the rampant beatings, rapes, killings. Doubts reared their heads in my mind like mushrooms. Was I, indeed, a fool and a traitor? Was I perhaps acting in the interest of white people who never loved blacks? Of what good was my activism to Junior? And to my mother? And to my friends, some of whom had taken the easier path of silence. Wasn't that easier path wiser?

"Suddenly I began to nurse the real hope of being released, of leaving that jungle alive, and becoming an important person in the Zanu-PF. I remembered Alexander Kanengoni, whose antiauthoritarian and humanistic writings had been inspirational but who became a supporter of Mugabe. I remembered professor Moyo, who once accused Mugabe of belittling universal issues of human rights, but who then supported Mugabe and even composed songs for his regime. What difference did their betrayal make? It changed nothing. Shouldn't I do the same if only for the benefit of my child?

"After these moments of doubt came a surge of new thought: life should be seen not as the absence of death. Rather it should be seen in the positive. I didn't know how I could live on if I denounced my convictions. I didn't know how I could still identify myself as a free person if I stood for nothing. Yet, should I die because of mere ideas? I became confused. I didn't know what to hold as truth: self preservation at all cost or belief in values that bind us and survive us all? Fits of mental blankness quickly gave way to moments of crystal sanity and then a momentary madness. My four years at the university, all the time I spent learning about ideas that have shaped the civilized world meant nothing to me anymore. Then I thought that it no longer made any difference whether I was alive or dead. As far as I was concerned, there was no longer any distinction between life and death in Zimbabwe. All the so-called sacrifices made by our anti-colonial fighters were no more than cow dung to me. I thought it was basically wrong for them to believe that we owed them our lives because they fought the colonial masters. It was wrong for Mugabe to identify himself with the fate of Zimbabwe. A country is always more than any individual.

"Having come to this thought, I was determined to go on the offensive the next time the commander wanted to convert me. I was prepared to challenge his and the other veterans' claim of our country as their birthright. When I was taken to his office for the next round of re-education, which wasn't different from the previous ones except that I was now asked pointedly whether I was finally ready to renounce the opposition and join the Mugabe camp, I recounted my genuine respect for Mugabe to which the commander assumed a self-congratulatory pose, nodding occasionally.

"It was then that I told him about one man called George Washington, a great commander, a war leader, and the first President of the United States of America. When he completed his two terms, he was asked to run for a third term, but he understood that the people were greater than he, an individual. He understood that the best legacy would be to leave office and make way for others to demonstrate their love of their country. I also reminded him of Nelson Mandela, who did not think that his 27 years in prison gave him the moral right to be president for life. That was it. Those thoughts of mine sealed my fate. Those words condemned me to death."

A deep sigh of shock rippled through the audience that seemed to awaken them from some kind of slumber. Even Yvonne momentarily stopped to write in her notebook and looked on, enraptured by Erica's narrative. Erica went on.

"When I discussed George Washington and Nelson Mandela, the veteran sprang from his chair as though stung by an ant. He left his office. That was the last time I saw him. Not long after he left, three armed men came, and saying nothing, led me out of the room and into a white van waiting outside. Two of them got in and the other joined the driver in front. I wasn't blindfolded so I could see where we drove. It was far deeper into a jungle whose location I couldn't identify. I suspected it was going to be my last journey. And it was.

"They pulled up to a clearing about the size of a tennis court. I alighted and they ordered me to strip naked. As I was doing that, I looked further to my left and saw a mound of freshly dug earth. One of them saw me glance at the mound. 'Yes,' he said. 'That's going to be your grave.'

"'But you can still save yourself,' another said.

"'Renounce the MDC,' the third added.

"'Come to Zanu-PF. Come back to Mugabe,' the first one said.

"I murmured to myself: '*Over my dead body.*'

"'Are you ready to save your life or not?' one of them asked.

"I didn't answer. It was cold. The sun was rapidly going down. It was being replaced by a somewhat dark cloud that seemed to quicken the otherwise sharp decline in temperature at this time of the year. The first man unzipped his trousers. That did not surprise me. The contrary would have. He had me. All of them had me.

"When the last person got off me, the first man ordered me to stand up. I did. He pointed at the ditch and told me to climb into it. I obeyed. They began to cover the ditch. I raised my voice to the oldest of them.

"'Please, save my life,' I begged. He said nothing. I reminded him that I had a son and that he had no one besides me. He murmured something that ended with 'your mother.' I knew that they found out that John was with my mother. I stopped begging.

"They covered the hole up to my neck, leaving my head to stick out. They left. I believed they would come back some hours later because I knew it was one of their terror methods. I had heard the veterans usually buried people to their necks for some hours to break their will. Usually, the person recanted his position when they returned. So, I believed they would come some hours later, or, at worst, the next day. But they did not.

"I spent the night in the jungle. The usual sharp drop in temperature was fiercer there. I thought my head was in a refrigerator. Ants crawled up and down my face freely. I shooed, blew air from my mouth and nose. That didn't help. Deep into the night harrowing noises clashed and clamored for attention. A lion could walk by, I thought. Or an anaconda. They wouldn't know what to do with my head, I thought, consoled by that. Somehow I fell asleep.

"Then it was day. The sun rose very early. It brought some warmth. I was sorely thirsty. I was ready to do anything just to have some drops of water on my tongue. I expected to hear some human voice. I desired it. That desire was even fiercer than thirst. None came. The sun grew hot and it poured right onto my face. It dazzled my sight so that I saw no more. I closed my eyes. I began to lose the awareness of my surroundings. Each time the duration was longer. Yet I hoped to hear the noise of a vehicle; I hoped to hear someone ask me whether I was ready to come back to Mugabe. It did not come. And then it was night. Night."

She stopped to take a breath. It was then that a voice drifted into the hall from outside as though eager to interrupt Erica's story. *"The horror, the horror!"*

Some people looked to the usual corner from where side comments had always come. An elderly bearded white man turned around and left. Erica kept silent, and when people turned back to look at her, she announced, "That was how I met my death."

"Oh, sister," sighed an elderly woman in the second pew by the left, wiping her tears. Many other women cried. But Erica was not touched by their tears. She did not lose her poise. Not at all. She apologized for having taken so long to tell her simple story and then turned to address Mugabe.

"Your excellency, sir, you were right in asking what Zimbabwe was to Britain." She turned back to the audience. "Isn't it time we asked him what Zimbabweans were to him?"

Having asked her question, she quietly walked back to her pew. People murmured curses toward Mugabe. Just about the time she got back, another woman came up to the front, stood and waited for attention, eager to tell her story. At the same time, Mugabe sprang to his feet, ready to challenge the mounting resentment hurled in his direction. "It's all lies. It's all lies," he shouted. "It's not true."

Equiano held his right palm outstretched toward Mugabe in a definite stop sign.

"But I have to defend myself," Mugabe said. "Don't I have the right to do so?"

"Of course, you do. This is not Zimbabwe. But you will have time to defend yourself. Let us first hear all the stories."

"I have to defend myself now," he shouted. "Now!"

Some people chuckled.

"But someone is already standing to tell her story," said the chief judge, pointing at the woman who had taken Erica's position. "Can you wait until we have heard her story?"

"It's all lies that Ms. Madai told here," Mugabe insisted.

"Not lies," said the woman standing at the front. "Her story is like mine. Just like mine. I was killed by the veterans."

"In this case, then," said Equiano, "you'd surely love to rebut both of them together."

"Kill two birds with one stone," Steve Biko said.

The compromise appealed to Mugabe and he sat down. Equiano conferred with the two other judges, then addressed the people. They would take only two more stories, then they would go on recess. After recess, Yvonne Vera would tell about *Gukurahundi* and then the judges would confer with God for His verdict. Since a woman was already standing, he suggested that the story coming after hers be told by a man, merely to keep some form of balance.

Dadirai Chipiro's Tears

Feeling that people's attention was still on Erica's story and that not many regarded her, the woman who came up to the front coughed loudly, and paced somewhat nervously, as if she were about to run back to her seat. Some people murmured in her direction. She looked up and was happy to see some eyes on her. "My name is Dadirai Chipiro," she said. "I am from Mhondoro district.

"The people around knew me as Mrs. Chipiro because of my husband. He was the head of the Movement for Democratic Change in our district. People loved him. They loved me. But, even though people loved us, I knew that the veterans would get us one day. And they got me. It was not very long ago. I died on Friday, June 6, 2008. This is my story.

"I was in my house preparing lunch when they came. Suddenly, I heard the noise of cars in front of our house. I thought my husband had come back home. But it wasn't him. It was not just one car. They were two. There were three men in each car. They wore army uniforms. When I saw the uniforms, my heart sank into a deep hole. I knew then that they had come for us. I could not run back into the house. I stood there like the pillar of salt in the Bible. My heart beat in my chest like our big village drum. I prayed. Please God, let them not see me. God of Israel, who gave the Egyptians plague, please, make them blind. Please, God, let them turn back. But they did not turn back. They did not become blind. They marched forcefully toward me, like soldiers in the war front. Their eyes were like hot coals. Their faces were like night masks. Their leader asked me, 'Woman, where is your husband?' I told them that he went to Harare. Another said, 'Harare, eh? For meeting of betrayers?' I said no. He went on an errand. Then I told them that he would be back later that day.

"Their leader told two of them to search for him in my house. They went in and searched. They did not find him. He was not there. I told them that I was telling the truth. But they did not leave me alone. No, they began to ask me many questions. They asked me whether I was a member of the opposition. I told them that I was not interested in politics. I was a simple housewife. They asked me whom I voted for in the election in March. I told them that I did not go to vote because I had a miscarriage. And that was true. So, they left.

"I was happy when they left. I was not interested in politics. I just supported my husband because he was my husband. But I was like many other women in our district who supported their husbands. Their sons and daughters have all left our country. All. They left because of hunger. Like these women, I wanted a different government. I wanted a government that could make the price of mealie meal more affordable again.

"Some people in the village came to know what they wanted. They told me I was lucky that the veterans didn't beat me. I knew I was lucky. Not many women were lucky. As we were still talking about these veterans we heard the same sound of vehicles I heard earlier. It was indeed the men. All of them came out of their cars. Their leader said that if I were the wife of a betrayer, I was therefore a betrayer. When I said nothing, they said that my silence was a sign of my guilt. And I had to suffer for that.

"They commanded the village people to stay. They tore off my clothes. They made me dirty. In front of village boys and girls. In front small children. My fellow women. I was crying. When they were done, they shot bullets in the air and told all to run away. They dragged me inside. One took out his machete and cut off my left arm. The pain was hell. I was shaking everywhere. My heart stopped. I was pleading. 'Please, please, have mercy. What did I do to you? Please have mercy.'

"But he did not have mercy. He cut the other hand. I was still crying. I was asking him to stop killing me. But he refused. He cut off my left leg. And then my right leg. I lay in my pool of blood, crying. I told them that God saw everything they did, and that God would judge them. But that did not get into their ears. I knew that they had no human hearts. Their hearts were stones. They left me naked in my pool of blood. I asked God to send somebody to take me to the hospital. No one came. But that was not the end of it. Suddenly smoke descended from the thatched roof. I saw flames falling on me. I wanted to run, but I had no hands and no feet. I could no longer breathe. Then, big fire swallowed me. I knew it was the end. I wanted to do the sign of the cross. But I had no hand. Then I prayed: 'God, please take my soul. Amen.'

"That is how I died. I didn't do anything to them. When Mugabe fought

44

against the white man who ruled us, all of us supported him. I, too, wanted the white people to leave us alone. I wanted us to rule ourselves. I did not want us to start killing ourselves. That is my story." She stared at the people. "That's all I have to say," she added with a slight genuflection.

A stark silence of disbelief shrouded Dadirai as she stood there, as though also in shock of her own story. "My story is not on YouTube. But many people know. I am sure it is in newspapers," she added as an afterthought and walked back to her pew as quietly as she had come to the front.

Yvonne turned her camera to Mugabe. He was casting angry glances in the direction Dadirai had gone. Dadirai was a betrayer. There was surely no other way Mugabe could have thought of her. Just then a baldheaded man in his late fifties walked up to the front and took Dadirai's place. Yvonne turned her camera to the man. She doubted whether his story would be as good as hers and Erica's. She had loved the down-to-earth, bone-wrenching stories told by women and she wished the next story teller was also a woman. Women, she knew, were the ultimate victims of *Guku Africanus.*

Footnote #3

What more can one say about *Guku*? Indeed, everything that needs to be said has been said. However, we believe there may be some who are interested in expanding this notion. We recommend that one even check the Wickipedia, actually Gukupedia. One could find some phrases such as:

temporary bouts of insanity

belief in the absolute goodness of one's world

Manichaean binary

the blunt refusal to emulate good ideas from other persons or parts of the world

culture of death such as exhibited by suicide bombers or those who inflict maximum injury on themselves in the belief that it harms their enemies

readiness to condemn others

other forms of negativities, etc.

The Strange But True Tale of Chenjerai Shiri, the War Veteran

The man who stepped forward ran his left hand over his bald head, hardly looking up to the audience that didn't seem yet ready for a new story. There was utter silence; despair was visible in most faces. Hadn't they already heard enough sad stories?

"I am standing here to say I'm sorry for my crimes," he announced in a choking voice. The sudden change in tenor of the pattern of storytelling lit up the people's faces. Surprisingly, this was not the story of a victim, but of a criminal. Is it possible that an African man would ever acknowledge his moral failings? That was good news and, encouraged by that, a voice shouted from one of the pews in the middle of the hall, "Go on, brother. Tell us, you are among your brothers and sisters."

"Thank you, brother," the bald headed, repentant criminal said, his voice regaining some balance. "I am here to say sorry to all those whose deaths I caused. They are not just two or three. They are many. But I hope you will understand and forgive me."

Mugabe shifted nervously in his seat, looked around his bodyguards as he wondered about this veteran who was going to spill the beans. The air in the hall was electrified with rapt attention. They were to get a firsthand account of the evil machinations of the Mugabe terror complex. "I join Erica to ask Mugabe the question she asked. But I also ask: What have we been to ourselves—we Zimbabweans? I don't know."

In a matter of minutes, the doubts and despair that originally showed on some people's faces gave way to sympathetic interest. They were truly ready to forgive this criminal. "My name is Chenjerai Shiri," he said.

A loud gasp followed his mention of his name. "No, no, not the person you think of," he quickly added. "I am not Hunzvi, not Perence," he clarified. "Those ones will have their own questions to answer."

The people were relieved to learn that they didn't have two of the most notorious names in Zimbabwean terror history in front of them. Nothing would have made them forgive those two. It would have been like asking Jews to forgive Dr. Mengele.

"I was a war veteran, a member of the Fifth Brigade," Chenjerai went on. As soon as he mentioned the Fifth Brigade, Yvonne, who had bit her lower lip to rein in her emotion, quickly bent to her notepad: *Fifth Brigade was to Ndebele what SS was to Jews*, she wrote.

"I sacrificed my life for our fatherland," Chenjerai said, sweeping the hall with his eyes. "Yes, I did. But people have already forgotten the sacrifice we veterans made for all of us."

"Don't accuse us, sir," a male voice shouted.

"I am not accusing any person," Chenjerai replied.

"When you say we have forgotten, it is an accusation," a young woman sitting beside Erica fired back. "Oh yes, it is."

Equiano hit his gavel twice on the table. "Give him the benefit of the doubt," he announced.

Chenjerai turned to him, nodded in thanks and returned to the woman who shouted at him. "Sorry, sister," he said. "I didn't intend my words to sound accusatory. I only wanted to state a historical fact. Our people have easily forgotten that we were ruled by white people just because they thought it fit to do so. They did it without our consent. We all agree on this, don't we?" he asked, turning to Mugabe whose face lit up like that of a child who has received a handful of bonbons.

Unable to contain his joy at the thought that Chenjerai, after all, was not a sell-out, Mugabe stood up. "Yes, tell them," he said, pride returning to his face. "We have to teach our people their history. That is what we are!"

By now the audience was totally confused. Wasn't Chenjerai a phony? Oh yes, he was. And he had come to play games with them. He solicited their understanding by confessing that he killed many people, yet he was now on Mugabe's side. But since the chief judge asked them to give him the benefit of the doubt, they had to listen. And so Chenjerai went on with his version of history: "Like Erica, I, too, am burdened by history. I have to remind us all what we have forgotten. We have forgotten that Cecil Rhodes' British South Africa Company gained permission from Queen Victoria to colonize our part of Africa. He called it Southern Rhodesia. It was Cecil Rhodes who said, 'I contend that we are the finest race in the world and the more of it we inhabit, the better.' He believed it was the white man's burden to bring Western civilization to other lands. I am a man of history, and this is what I remember."

For the first time, Mugabe was sincerely smiling. He had good teeth! Actually a handsome man.

"In the good year of the Lord, 1922, which was bad for us," Chenjerai proceeded, "the British South African administration ended. By then, a number of British people had already begun to consider our land theirs and they opted for independence from Britain. That was the beginning of white minority rule in our homeland. In the good year of the Lord, 1930, which was bad for us, the white minority rule enacted the Land Appointment Act. Our people finally lost their lands and became visitors in their homelands. So, our great men and women formed an army to fight them. They were Bishop Abel Muzorewa, Ndabaningi Sithole, Joshua Nkomoh, Robert Gabriel Mugabe, and others. Of these strong sons of the soil, the strongest and the most cunning was Robert Gabriel Mugabe, who understood the whites very well. He fought them and became our hero."

Even against their inclination, people applauded Mugabe as a hero. And, having already lost himself in transcendent smiles, he stood up to acknowledge the accolades that he deserved. At the height of the applause, another group of figures sauntered by. But they did not spend much time. Nor did they say anything. They strolled on, perhaps to peep at another trial going on elsewhere.

"I'm sorry to remind you that there was a thing called apartheid," Chenjerai went on.

"Tell them," said Mugabe.

"It was a white-only regime in South Africa. A regime designed to put blacks as foreigners in their homelands. But honorable men and women of South Africa rose against it. They fought against racism and against inhumanity. Steve Biko paid with his life."

He made a hand movement in the direction of Steve Biko, who showed no reaction. "Mandela sacrificed 27 years of his life in prison," he went on. "Thabo Mbeki was a formidable fighter in the ANC liberation front in Angola. He was the architect of all plans. From Angola, he, together with other fighters, launched attacks on the vicious regime of South Africa. But the South African army was very strong. Remember, they were supported by Britain, the USA, and Israel. So their powerful army came into Namibia and got into Angola. They were about to conquer the ANC liberation front stationed there. They had a specific order to kill Thabo Mbeki. That would have meant the end of the very strong anti-apartheid movement. But God was on their side. That was in early 1980s. Those of us with good memories can still remember. God had already liberated Zimbabwe and put it in the hands of its rightful owners, in the hands of black people, in the hands of our hero, Robert Gabriel Mugabe."

Mugabe nodded. At the same time, many faces were tightening with concern. No doubt, Chenjerai was determined to upend the trial; his recitation dovetailed into Mugabe's narrative of Zimbabwe. And for Mugabe, there was no doubt that the world was beginning to understand him and, soon, the so-called trial would fizzle, rightfully ignoring his nemesis, *Guku*. Some people even began to believe that he would soon go scot-free. Others, however, were sure that nothing would prevent Mugabe from going to where he belonged: hell. So, they hoped and listened.

"When Thabo Mbeki knew no other place to run to, Robert Mugabe opened the doors and gates of Zimbabwe for him and his army. Brothers and sisters, can you imagine how beautiful it is when a black brother falls into the arms of another black brother while fleeing white enemies? That was it. Mbeki knew he was safe. I was there. I saw it with my naked eyes.

"I was a 30-year-old soldier then. For the first time in my life, I felt hot tears in my eyes. Tears of joy. For 14 long years, Mugabe protected South African freedom fighters. For 14 long years, he fed them. He gave them arms. He gave them moral support, told them that their fight was for a just cause."

Yvonne's face had become longer than usual. Consternation and fury had weighed down her lips which formed an unusual "W" shape. She had known it, she thought to herself. Only women's stories were down-to-earth realistic. But, well, since they were there to collect evidence, Chenjerai's account might, after all, not be out of place. In every trial, every piece of evidence should be considered and there was no reason Mugabe's positive contributions to the African anti-imperialist struggle should be ignored. That, surely, was the silver lining in the dark clouds of Chenjerai's story. And so, she turned her whole attention to Chenjerai, who proudly recited his knowledge of Zimbabwean history.

"I was one of the soldiers in charge of defending Mbeki. I was ready to sacrifice my life for him because I knew that what he was fighting for was greater than all of us. Can you imagine what could have happened if he had been killed? Mandela could have been killed as well. South Africa would still be under apartheid. Isn't that so?"

"Rhetoric!" shouted a male voice, obviously no longer ready to give Chenjerai the benefit of the doubt.

"It's not rhetoric. It is history," Chenjerai fought back. "Are you telling me that white people are innocent?" he asked.

"Some white people also fought against apartheid," said another voice. "Helen Suzman. Denis Brutus."

"Well, just a few," Chenjerai grunted. "It was the fault of South Africa. They attacked us because we were supporting our brothers. In August 1981, they destroyed our military base in Inkomo. In June 1982, the South African army carried out an abortive attack on Mugabe's residence."

"Tell us about how you died," said an elderly, white-haired man. "That's why you are here."

"Who killed you?" a voice asked.

"What killed you?" came yet another voice.

Chenjerai looked up, stared at Mugabe, who was chuckling to himself. He cleared his throat for attention, and looked in the direction of Erica: "I died of Veteran Disease," he said glumly and fell into a deep silence.

After a long while a voice whispered. "Tell us, brother. Who did it to you?"

"No person did anything to me," he replied, seemingly emboldened by the acknowledgment of his guilt. "I did things to people. To women. I was told to do so. I was told it was part of war."

Yvonne nervously pushed aside some strands of her braids that blocked her sight. Perhaps Chenjerai was repentant after all.

"Our first enemies were white people. We knew that the war has not yet been won until they left our land. Our commanders told us that a soldier was not yet

51

a true soldier until he raped a woman. To rape a white woman was the highest honor, because white people were our greatest enemies. Those who supported them were the second-greatest enemies. Those who did not support us were the third-greatest enemies. When the land became ours, we began to pay back our greatest enemies in their own coin. Whites. They deserved it. Their men raped our women.

"I had never been interested in white women but I was made to try it once. It was like taking a bitter pill that will make you well. I was told it was like a ritual hardening. I knew I wouldn't enjoy lying over a white woman, but I did it. Yes, I forced myself into her.

"But that was only once. Just that once. I know you want to know how it happened. This is how it happened: we were three veterans. We ambushed them a couple of miles off their farm. It was a family—a man and his wife and a teenage girl. We came out of the bush. We tied the man's hand and legs. We did not want to kill him because he was not armed. We just wanted to have his women. We dragged the two in the bush. They did not resist at all. They begged us not to do it to them. The girl's whisper broke my heart. 'Please, please, please, don't do it, don't do it.'

"I didn't do it to her. The other veterans did. It was her mother I raped. She did not whimper or cry like her daughter did. No, she merely looked on, speechless, as I did it to her. She looked me in the eye all the time. Naked on the ground, she held her hands to her breasts, looking at me while I forced my way in. Those green eyes of hers. They saw my heart. My heart started to beat like it never had before. Not even while in the jungle facing a lion did my heart shake as it did when that innocent woman looked at me while I was on her. I didn't eat for two days. Whenever I recalled her green eyes, green like the leaves of a plant, I shuddered. Then I swore never to do it to white women. And I never did it again. But my companions did—it gave them kicks. They ambushed them. They raided their homes. Rape, rape, rape. They raped white women for the pride of it."

"This is propaganda," Mugabe shouted.

"No, your excellency," Chenjerai said, turning sharply to him. "It is not propaganda. We did it. It is part of our history. History. We are our history. We veterans raped white women. That was what we were told to do. That was how to get back at the white man. It was you who ordered it."

"Shut up there!" Mugabe went on.

"No, I cannot. It was you, your excellency, who ordered it."

He turned to the audience; some held their hands to their mouths in shock, while some were gleeful at the turn of the veteran's narrative.

"Erica talked about *pungwe* camps. There were many of them. I led one of them, in the early years of our independence, in Hwange, a beautiful town not far from Victoria Falls. Hwange is tucked in the midst of forests, and our *pungwe* camp was there. I spent the first night with two virgins, 16 years old. One was from Nyamandlovu and the other was from Tsholotsho.

"They spent three weeks with me. Then they were moved over to the boys for their initiation into the revolution.

"After those girls, I stopped spending many nights with the same women. I had a different woman every night. In my first year, I went for the untouched. But there were soon no more untouched."

He shrugged. "Well, other veterans also preferred virgins. So, we had to make do with whatever came. 20-year-old, 30, sometimes some 40-year-old women, depending on their condition. Our young boys were happy. They looked forward to it. It was their nightly reward for their hard daily training. If any girl got pregnant she was sent home. We wanted many Zanu-PF children."

"All Ndebele girls?" a voice asked.

"Yes, Ndebele girls," Chenjerai confirmed. "After all, Mzilikazi did it to our women many years ago."

"So, it was vengeance," Marechera asked.

"He told us it was justice."

"He? Who is he?" Biko interjected, after which Chenjerai turned to Mugabe.

"You wanted justice from white people and from tribes other than yours?" Biko pressed on. Chenjerai kept a short silent and knowing no better defense, went on with his story as if nothing had happened.

"The post-independence *pungwe* lasted about five years. We disbanded the camps when the dissidents in the South were defeated and the peace treaty was signed in 1987. The re-education in the camps brought Zimbabwe back to its path to salvation, to unity and progress. We lived in peace and prosperity. But we knew our enemies would never rest. Enemies never sleep. The white South Africans did not like the idea that a black country like Zimbabwe was doing well. So they sought a way to destabilize us. That was the origin of the opposition party called MDC. It was the creation of White South Africa and Britain.

"We knew that. Their leader, Morgan Tsvangirai had met with British leaders and was beginning to confuse many people. We had to act to maintain order in our country. I was called to apply my knowledge of the post-independence *pungwe*. That was in 2000. I went to the Mutare. We began a re-education of the supporters of Tsvangirai.

"Rape of women?" a female voice asked.

"Teaching them to behave," he responded. "They were sell-outs. They brought it upon themselves."

"They gave you AIDS?" one voice asked.

He breathed deeply and looked around like a child caught lying. "I thought that AIDS didn't kill," he proceeded in a lower tone of voice. "They told us it was a white man's disease. It had nothing to do with Africans. They told us it was the disease of the morally decadent, of homosexuals and those who practiced sodomy. They told us it was the disease of those who have gone against nature. We believed veterans were strong. We survived many things in the jungle—snake bites, scorpion and bee stings, gonorrhea, syphilis, and other silly things. If we survived them, there was nothing we could not survive. We believed it all. And we went on with our veteran lives.

"When a doctor told me that I was HIV-positive, I did not believe it would lead to my death. But when I began to thin away like a sick dog it became clear to me. The doctor told me I had just about a year more to live. It was then that I knew I had been deceived. I had been used."

He stopped as though fighting tears. He shook his head glumly. "I am sorry for all the women I slept with...all of them."

"So you were part of those who killed Ndebele people," Equiano said.

"Indirectly. I did not shoot any innocent people. No, I never shot an innocent person."

"Who shot them?" Biko asked.

"Other members of the Fifth Brigade."

"Did Mr. Mugabe know that they were shooting innocent people?" Marechera asked.

"Yes, he knew about it. He told us that it was the only way to root out the dissidents. Their people hid them and they had to pay for that."

"And the army killed thousands of them," Marechera went on.

"Yes."

"Even though there were only a few hundred dissidents," Marechera pursued.

"Would you call the killing genocide?" Biko asked.

Chenjerai hesitated, but quickly overcoming his vacillation, nodded. "Yes, it was genocide. But I was not part of it. I didn't kill any innocent person."

"Yes, you did," a woman shouted.

"Thou shall not condemn," Equiano said, turned to Chenjerai and dismissed him with a flick of the hand. He announced to the audience that they could go for recess.

Footnote #4

This is a very short animal tale told to a group of uninterested African children by an African elder who has seen generations of Africans pass by and worlds fall apart, but does not know how to explain all he has seen to younger generations, and therefore has grown disillusioned, and is now about to die.

"Once upon a time—and what a long time ago it was—that was before the earth became what it now is, way before the shell of tortoises became as hard as they now are and human beings began to talk as they now do, a skunk and a rat went to hunt. Shouldn't we say that skunks and rats used to be very close family members? Yes, they used to be, but then something happened along the way and they finally went apart.

"They stole into a rich man's house and chanced on a roasted quail the man was preparing to serve to his noble guests. When they saw the piece of meat they rejoiced and said to themselves, 'Hurrah, we shall eat ourselves to dizziness.' As soon as they had said so, they began to nibble at the delicious treat as much as they could. And then they were satisfied. They stored enough meat in their mouth for their loved ones and left for home. On their way back, they forgot the route through which they had entered the house. They eventually found a way out, but unknown to them, the way they chose led to a ditch into which liquid ammonia had been poured out by the rich man who happened to be an alchemist. Oh, we should have said it earlier. The rich man was indeed an alchemist.

"So, the skunk and the rat fell into the smelly little ditch. Luckily for them, though, they managed to get out, but, gosh, how they smelled. *Uhh!* The rat said to the skunk, 'Hey, brother, we smell like garlic in an unwashed mouth. What should we do about this?'

"But the skunk countered, 'Eh, bro, you're always too anxious about how you look. What is wrong with you?'

"The rat said to the skunk, 'Smell your armpit.'

"The skunk did. He frowned and said, 'Nothing. I do not smell.'

"'Mine smells,' the rat said.

"'Ah, it is all in your mind.'

"But the rat knew what he was talking about and no sooner had he said it than he saw a small stream. He said to the skunk, 'Bro, I'm going to have a bath whether you like it or not.' Then he dove into the stream and took a thorough bath. The skunk, happy that he had fed well and oblivious to the way he smelled, kept on his way home. The rat, meanwhile, washed himself and caught up with the skunk so that they walked back home together. Meanwhile the skunk's smell was rising up to the heavens, gosh!

"When they arrived home, the skunk's wife, who was pregnant, went to meet her husband, but as soon as she came near, she perceived the breath-stopping acrid odor and said, 'Hey, dearest, you smell. What happened to you?'

"The skunk was highly offended and barked at his wife, 'Don't be like the rat. How can you say that I smell? Are you mad? I do not smell.'

"But his wife said, 'Please go and take your bath. You should get the smell off your body.'

"'Shut up, woman,' the skunk shouted. 'Don't tell your husband what he should do.'

"But his wife insisted and told him what she heard carried by the wind. She said, 'I heard that we are approaching the twelfth hour at which God will make everything permanent. If you don't wash off your dirt now, you will smell forever. I will live alone if you don't wash up.'

"'So you're going to leave me because the rat told you I smell?'

"'No, I know that you smell. That is why I am saying it.'

"'You have been brainwashed by the rat, woman.'

"The skunk's wife began to vomit because she could not stand the smell. And while she threw up, she experienced pain in her lower abdomen and soon her water broke. Since there was no one to help but her husband, she had to put up with her his skunky smell while giving birth to their children, who, overwhelmed by the odoriferous presence of their dad, also began to smell. It was a few seconds to midnight, the time when God would make everything permanent. Having gone through the difficult pain of birth, and having given birth to nine little skunks, Frau Skunk no longer distinguished between good and bad smell because even her children also smelled like their dad.

"The next day, the skunk asked the rat to go hunting together, but the rat answered, 'No, I'm not going with you. Your smell makes one throw up.'

"Again, the skunk was offended. Sad and mad, he said to the rat, 'Don't insult me.'

"But the rat insisted, 'No, no, I will no longer go hunting with you.'

"But the skunk said, 'I do not smell. Even if I smell, it is not my fault. I am not to blame. It is the rich man who poured ammonia into that ditch who should be blamed.'

"And so they no longer hunted together. They were no longer friends because the skunk became skunk and smelled and lived like skunk."

Part Two

Gukurahundi
1980-1987

Interlude

The recess appeared more than earned. Like the school children at the ring of the recreation bell, the audience dispersed the moment the chief judge announced that the court was now on a break. The speedy disappearance from the hall left behind a ricocheting emptiness, and a treacherous silence. One person who sat on her pew was like a dot in the vast grayness of the enormous trial hall.

Yvonne, a dot?

Surely she was much more than that, for she wasn't a small woman at all. In the graceful fullness of her serene African womanhood, she couldn't be called a dot. She was a huge question mark. Yes, she was, at least judging from how she hunched over her notebook, with pen in her right hand, thinking.

A number of questions had collected in her mind; most prominent was Chenjerai's admission that the killings in Matabeleland was genocide. She had been uncomfortable with the word, had avoided mentioning it in her novel. The nearest she came to naming what happened in Matabeleland in the early 1980s was merely calling Kezi a graveyard. She even refrained from using the word *Gukurahundi*, which would have alerted the world that what Mugabe had in mind was nothing short of ethnic cleansing.

No less weighty in her mind was how to tell the story of the stone virgins when court resumed. To her, and her alone, belonged the second part of the trial. How best could she tell the stories? Would this demanding audience be patient enough with the abundant lyricism of her original narrative? Surely, they want meaty, juicy details. Perhaps she should just meet with the two sisters and urge them to tell their stories, since they were there, to speak for themselves. Was it ethical to tell a person's story while the individual was there?

59

This question lingered disturbingly long in her mind given that she was a person of high ethical standards. In the end, however, she remembered what she learned in one of her literature classes while she was a graduate student in Canada. Stories do not belong to individuals; they belong to communities. They belong to humanity. What a beautiful thought. She smiled as she remembered Leslie Marmon Silko, the originator of the idea, when she visited her school. Stories that deal with the human condition belong to every human being. Everyone has the right to tell stories regardless of who their original owners are. They are common property. By the same token, the injustice done to one person is done to all. When Thenjiwe was raped, the whole world was raped and when she died, the world died with her. Yvonne was happy for this thought and she nodded to herself; to tell her story was to tell Zimbabwe's story. It was to tell the story of every woman who was raped, and every man who was denied his justice. To tell how Nonceba found love even in the midst of war was to tell about the fundamental thirst for human warmth in every soul.

Satisfied with her reflection so far, Yvonne no longer believed it necessary to have the sisters tell their stories. Rather she felt emboldened enough to step forward and humbly tell them. She would have to rethink the stories, and tell them in such a way that the sisters would listen as if the stories were no longer theirs.

Merely tickling her mind while waiting for inspiration, she underlined the title she wrote down before the beginning of the trial: *The Trial of African Octogenarian Dictators, Part I.* However, on second thought, she crossed it out, knowing right away that it was too general. There were too many African dictators for a single discourse to cover. In fact, if people were to write about them, the books would stand taller than Mount Kilimanjaro. She needed to be very particular, indeed; tell the story of the dictator she knew very well. Just one. The second title that came to her mind did the trick: *The Trial of Robert Mugabe.*

She was happy with the aptness of this title. She remembered what she used to teach budding writers: write about what you know. Characters are people, human beings. Period! Write about them as if you were in the same place. Bring them to life. "How great life could be if only we kept it simple," she murmured and was surprised to hear some chuckle escape her mouth. It reminded her of her young self in Kezi, when Zimbabwe was still Africa's Eden. Ah, those good old times.

To remind herself of the seriousness of her next task, she threw a glance at the place where Mugabe had been. That man needed to hear how people suffered under his regime. *But how do I begin to tell a story as complex as Guku?* she thought and went on with her sketch. "One family's story," she wrote, intending it to be a subtitle, but then cancelled it, knowing it wasn't good enough. She went on to write down ideas that could help her develop the story: how the members of a particular family lost their lives in the post-independence genocide in Matabeleland.

What, by the way, happened to Thenjiwe and Nonceba's parents in the original story? They just disappeared without much explanation. People need to know what happened to them. Round off the family to five: Papa, Mama, Thenjiwe, Nonceba and, perhaps another child—probably a son. Since Mama couldn't bear a son, let her adopt one for the family. Sounds good. Poetic license.

She held her lips together as if to hold her sketch. But her mind couldn't let go of the last two words she murmured to herself. *Poetic license.* She felt guilty for using them, yet she went on to justify them. *I have the license to tell stories in such a way that they convey the human experience,* she thought. *People must know what happened in Kezi.* She drew another line under the title, and then moved down a paragraph and wrote:

The Gumede Family

Dumiso, father (Age: mid-60s)

Sihle, mother (Age: late 50s)

Thenjiwe, daughter (Shorten to Thenji. Age: 23)

Nonceba, daughter (Shorten to Nonce. Age: 20)

Mlamuli, an adopted son (Age: 17).

To remind herself of some of the golden rules of storytelling, she wrote a note of warning: Don't get bogged down in minutiae. Take care of the audience. Just let them see the place where people died. Their imagination will do the rest. Keep It Simple, Sincere.

She glanced at her watch. The recess will still last a while, enough time to picture the Gumede family and accompany the members to their deaths. To help her picture Kezi and the events, she wrote down one of the memorable lines from her novel. *Kezi is a cemetery. To die here is to be abandoned to vultures and unknown graves.*

That written, she remembered two pregnant young women who were shot to death and disemboweled on the banks of the Cewale River in Lupane by the members of the Fifth Brigade. Goose bumps rushed to her skin and she shook her head, reminding herself not to be taken in by emotion. Mlamuli knew one of those young women. Yes, he did, she said to herself and closed her eyes, happy to see Mlamuli in his own environment.

Mlamuli

Mlamuli Robert Gumede walked with a limp, thanks to the polio he had as a child. His limp was compounded by yet another childhood ailment that also left its mark: chickenpox. At the centre of his forehead was a dark spot. Right over his left brow was another, and beneath the right eye was yet another. On his right cheek there were another dozen tiny, dim blotches on his already proudly dark skin.

At Kezi primary school, children giggled and ridiculed him: *Leper, leper, Mlamuli the Leper*. His two elder sisters, Thenji and Nonce, were already finished with school by the time he began, so he was alone to swim through the harsh waters of primary schools full of niggling fishes, not big enough to devour, but so effective with their guerrilla attack of hit and run. To avoid them, he slunk into corners during recess. But even there, some children still sought him out for ridicule.

Mlamuli's fortunes began to change one day when two boys found him hiding behind one of the three big marula trees that stood a bit removed from the classroom block. "Here he is. The leper," one of them whispered loudly, pointing at him. The other cackled. "Mlamuli the leper."

At the same time, three girls about the same age as Mlamuli walked by. One of them, a fair, chubby girl, quickly intervened. "Stop that," she screamed at the boys.

Mlamuli stood, rooted to the spot, his eyes running nervously between the boys and the girls. The cowardly boys took a few steps backward, which encouraged the plump girl to hammer them with reproach. "You don't do that. Don't be bad to others," she preached. To underline the importance of her message, she dipped her hands in the pockets of her skirt, but finding nothing, she produced the bonbon she had put into her mouth a while ago, halved it with her teeth and extended half to Mlamuli. "Take it," she said. "It's for you."

Her two friends looked on, surprised. As did Mlamuli. Was she merely mocking him? But he took the bonbon, running his eyes from his Good Samaritan to her two friends and a few other pupils who had gathered. "It's for you," she said. "Eat it."

He threw it into his mouth.

"My name is Sarah," she went on.

Just then, two fair, plump boys a bit older than Sarah forced their way through the small group. Without wasting a glance on Mlamuli, one of them pulled her away. She struggled. "You're hurting me, Mathew," she cried, freeing her hand from his grip. The other boy joined. Yet Sarah didn't budge. "Leave me alone," she yelled as she wriggled free.

"He's a leper," Mathew said.

"He's not," Sarah retorted and walked back to Mlamuli, who stood as though fixed to the ground. During the next day's recess, Sarah found him hiding behind a chimanimani shrub. She was accompanied not by her two girlfriends, but by her twin brothers. They apologized to Mlamuli for their unruly behavior the previous day and extended their mother's invitation to their house.

What might have begun as Sarah's innocent move to aid a boy bullied by others was the beginning of a long friendship and, for Mlamuli, a new life. He knew no other girl, not even when they went to Njube High School where he excelled in academics. The friendship went beyond the two. Mlamuli's acceptance into the Ndlovu family didn't come without hesitation, though. The Ndlovus were Anglicans, while Mlamuli was Catholic. But Mary, Sarah's mother, a Shona, was raised a Catholic. Beyond her naturally easy disposition toward others, she was happy to welcome a Catholic into her household. With time, Mlamuli became like a family member.

In their adolescence, Sarah and Mlamuli witnessed not only the transformation of their homeland from British colony to an independent country, but also their bodies. They found joy in the beauty of their differences and appeared even further soldered together by a force neither understood, nor cared to. In tune with the wisdom and care that such subtle discoveries brought, they learned to keep the warmth they felt toward each other to themselves.

And so Mlamuli became sure of the beauty and sanity of their world. He was sure of the place of Zimbabwe in God's mind until Mathew and George disappeared from their lives after they were forcefully conscripted into the band of Ndebele dissidents. Mlamuli could surely have been drafted, were it not for his spindly leg.

◆◆

Mlamuli never imagined that the moment he threw Sarah's half-eaten bonbon into his mouth, the very second her saliva mixed with his and his tongue glided where hers had, their fate would be tied like tendrils to a tree. His pain became hers and hers entirely his. He felt Mathew and George's recruitment intensely. While Jerome and Mary hoped their sons would soon return, Mlamuli wouldn't be consoled. He carried the pain on his young face as if that alone gave meaning to his life.

He wasn't alone in this though. Every second face in Kezi was like that wall upon which the period's *menetekel* was written. Mugabe's electoral win was seen as the ultimate triumph of the Shona people, and that allowed the Ndebele dissidents to claim right of resistance. The Ndlovu family felt the ensuing conflict not only because their sons were now dissidents, but also because one of the dissidents had remarked that Mary was a Shona and that she had been heard criticizing them. It was true. But she wasn't the only one to utter negative comments about the Ndebele dissidents. As a Shona by birth, however, hers fell into the tribal fault line. Mary knew she was no longer safe and went into hiding—in the attic.

The dissidents didn't come in the day. They came at night. They banged at the door, demanding it be opened. Jerome calmly opened the door. Two masked, armed men forced themselves in. Brushing aside Jerome, his daughter, and Mlamuli, they stomped in, their heads turning from one corner of the sitting room to another in search of what only they knew. A third armed man entered and immediately yelled, "Where is your wife?"

"She is not here," Jerome responded in a calm voice.

"Don't tell us lies. Where is she?"

"She went to see her mother."

The other two dashed into different rooms, upturned beds, opened every cupboard in search of Mary.

"When did she go to her mother?" the soldier asked.

"This afternoon."

"No one left this village today. Someone saw her this evening. Where is she?"

Soon, the other two came back to the parlor and reported that they didn't see her. But the interrogator was cocksure about his opinion. "You hid her," he told Jerome. "You have to tell us where she is."

"I have told you where she is," Jerome said. But hardly did the last word come out of his mouth when the interrogator punched him in the stomach.

"Why are you beating me?" he asked, hardly losing his composure. That had no impact on the interrogator, who told him they knew that Mary was somewhere nearby and that he would see to it that she appeared that night. With that, he turned to the other men and told them to teach Jerome a lesson. They happily complied, using the butts of their rifles and their boots on him.

Sarah hid her face in Mlamuli's chest and cried. That attracted the attention of the interrogator. He yanked her from Mlamuli's arms and pulled her toward him so that she fell into his arms. Mlamuli limped forward in protest. "Leave her alone," he yelled. "She did nothing to you. Leave her."

The commander sneered, gave Mlamuli's spindly leg a wicked kick so that he spun around clockwise, shouting with pain and fell on the ground. The man ripped Sarah's shirt and bra apart baring her breasts. Now, sure of her fate, Sarah begged for mercy. "Please don't do it. Please, please."

No longer capable of silently witnessing the pain in her house, Mary opened the secret chamber and called out to the dissidents. They should take her, rather than beat her family any more. They stopped beating Jerome and ordered him to provide a ladder to bring Mary down.

The commander dragged Sarah into Mathew's room. Mlamuli's efforts to save his love were met with a calm but determined warning. "If you stand up, I'll shoot you," he commanded, pointing his gun at his head. He lay on the floor, his pain aggravated by Sarah's cry. The men blindfolded Mary and Jerome, tied their hands behind them, and led them away.

With pain pulsating in his leg and head and, unable to stand on his own, Mlamuli crawled into Mathew's room. Sarah lay on the floor in the left corner, curled into fetal position. Her buttocks and the back of her thighs were smeared with blood.

"Sarah," he called. Hardly was her name called when she moved away, covering her ears with her arms, forming a V with her elbows pointed to the wall. A surge of hate and regret choked Mlamuli. If only he had been a man. He inched toward her. But the moment he touched her, she jerked, drew away from him.

"Go away. Go away. Go!" she cried, suddenly balling her two hands together in front of her chest so her wrists protected her breasts.

Mlamuli didn't go away; he mechanically reached for the wraparound cloth on Mathew's bed and placed it on Sarah. She grabbed the cloth and covered herself without turning to him. "Sarah," he called, crying. "They took them away."

Sarah quickly turned her face to him.

"They took your parents."

She stared for a while and then began to sob.

"I am sorry, Sarah," Mlamuli said, still afraid to touch her.

Sarah dragged herself out of the room, hardly raising her legs from the floor. Mlamuli followed her as though he feared she would crumble at the next step.

♦♦

Mlamuli took Sarah to his parents' house. She had become a member of Gumede family in the same way he had been a member of hers. Hardly getting half the details of what happened, Sihle, a tall and lean woman in her mid-fifties, cursed Matabeleland and Zimbabwe and soldiers and war. Then she fell into a deep well of silence, just as her daughters had. Dumiso was never one for many words. Averting his eyes from his crying wife and daughters and, as though ashamed of letting his son know that he too had emotions, he quietly wiped his eyes.

In and around Gumede's family was a silence as huge as the night, a fear as solid and dark as the sacred Mbelele cave. It wasn't much different from the fear that had gripped Matabeleland in the past months, not different from the shock of other random acts of violence by the dissidents. Unable to fathom what was happening to them, people were left with only the why-questions. Why are people so evil? Why are they doing this to us? They were questions they knew would never be answered. In the absence of answers, however, they began to weave solidarity with the victims of man's inhumanity to man. Each time Sihle hugged Sarah, her tears poured forth. "Sorry, my daughter. Sorry," she whispered. Thenji and Nonce slept with Sarah in the same room and did their best to show her she was not alone. They convinced Mlamuli that Sarah's silence and her cringe from him wasn't directed against him and that he wasn't a failure, contrary to his shame.

A couple of months after the rape, the probable became certain. Sarah's condition could no longer be denied. And that compounded her feeling of filth. She wasn't good enough to live. Sihle and her daughters assured her that she was as good as any person and that they would help her take care of her child. Eager to demonstrate his love, Mlamuli promised her that the two would begin a normal life together when things died down; they would be parents to that child.

But things were probably never going to die down. Indeed, they were just beginning to be out of their hands. A little more than three months after Sarah's pregnancy began to show to casual observers, the prime minister spelled out his way of dealing with the dissidents. He planned to address the nation on that issue, for he had now made up his mind. On the evening of the address, the Gumede family circled around their brown Philips transistor to hear about their fate.

"Fellow countrymen. It has come to our notice that certain people in Matabeleland fail to appreciate our journey toward freedom. They call themselves the opposition or dissidents. But we know who they are. They are the instruments of British Empire. Let me make it clear to them: Zimbabwe is a free country! We shall never become a British colony again. The situation in Matabeleland is one that requires a change. The solution is a military one. To the dissidents we say, watch out. *Kupura mhunga kana rukweza.* The rain is coming to wash away the hundi. We have started a great offensive, called Operation Gukurahundi. Our Fifth Brigade, trained to deal with dissidents, will do the job. We shall eradicate the dissidents. We shall root them out. We shall fight. And when we fight, we won't differentiate. Watch out! We don't tell who is a dissident and who is not. This will be the final solution to our nagging

68

problem. Long live *chimurenga*. Long live Zimbabwe. *A luta continua*!"

Dumiso, already lean, suddenly appeared drained, as if he had lost several pounds in the seconds following the announcement. Staring into an empty space, his lips moved as if of their own accord. "So we are the rubbish to be swept away," he murmured.

Sihle was rather optimistic. "There will be no war," she suggested. "They will be after only the dissidents."

"They will not attack us," Thenji agreed.

A couple of weeks after Mugabe's announcement, news of the devastations wrought by the Fifth Brigade in Tsholotsho rippled throughout Matabeleland. The Fifth Brigade walked through Tsholotsho like the angels of plague did in the land of Egypt. The soldiers all wore red berets and drove in funny-looking vehicles. They spoke Shona and sang songs in praise of the revolution and killed people like one killed flies. To some, the details of the news were largely too grotesque to be believed. Some even doubted that there were red-beret wearing soldiers. Even if there were such soldiers, they couldn't possibly kill innocent people. Many people nonetheless took precautionary steps, sneaking out of their houses very early in the morning and moving into the nearby jungles.

Dumiso traveled to Antelope Mine, as he had always done at the end of month, to receive his monthly pension. He did this despite his wife's apprehension about the situation in their land. It was too dangerous to travel, she cautioned. That wasn't a strong enough argument to sway him from going for his pension. Like the elderly men of his age, he never bought the idea of hiding in the jungle. But he encouraged his wife and children to do so. If, however, the soldiers should catch them, Mlamuli should tell them that he was named after the prime minster. It was true: many families named their sons after Robert Gabriel Mugabe, the freedom fighter who was thrown into prison without trial. "Tell them that your name is Robert," Dumiso said. "They will understand."

If only he were sure his words were true!

Three days past the date Dumiso was supposed to be back, Sihle could no longer bear the anxiety of awaiting his return. She was determined to search for him, despite her children's opposition. Thenji offered to accompany her.

"No," Sihle said. "They might be on the road."

"That is why we don't want you to go, Mama," Thenji said.

"I have to find my husband," she insisted. "Take care of your sister and your brother and Sarah. They come late morning and in the afternoon," she reminded her and went on to assure them that she knew where to hide at Antelope Mine. She, too, used to work at the Antelope Park, not far from the gold mines.

Sarah never felt well as she spent her days in the jungle. She vomited occasionally, held her hands to her stomach to calm the child inside her. One morning, she felt so dizzy that she didn't even get out of bed. There was no way she would drag herself to the jungle. And she didn't want Mlamuli to risk his life by taking care of her as he had offered. She urged him to flee with his sisters, but he wouldn't. "I can't leave you alone," he insisted, sitting at the edge of her bed.

"They will kill you if they come," she argued.

"I don't look like a dissident, do I? I can't leave you alone here. What if you die before they come?"

"I will not die. It's just the baby. It moves," she said. "I'll be okay."

Visibly pleased, yet disturbed by their brother's decision, Thenji and Nonce hoped that Mlamuli's misshapen leg and Sarah's pregnancy wouldn't look interesting to the soldiers. So, they wished them well and left for their hiding place.

Mlamuli felt woozy the moment his sisters left. For the first time in his life, he felt the burden of responsibility in his gut. He felt the burden of having to truly defend a defenseless person, a pregnant woman who needed the protection of a man. But was he a man? Not even if he had two healthy legs. No, not in the face of *Gukurahundi*. He calmly walked out of her room into the parlor where he paced, praying that that day would go by uneventfully. "God, God, keep them away from us!" Yet something told him they would come that day. It was a voice. Or was it the hollowness within, the idiotic humming in his head? Stepping to the front of the house, he understood what Kezi felt like when they all were in the jungle. It was a haunted village, disturbingly quiet.

A few minutes before noon, that silence grew hands and feet and eyes and peered inside Mlamuli. Perhaps some ghosts patrolled the village. Dogs barked.

70

Did they see them? Cocks cackled and goats bleated nervously. Did they anticipate what was to come? Or was it already here? Sure, the angels of death were around. Their gunshots sounded afar. Mlamuli hurried back to Sarah and shook her awake. "Sarah, Sarah, they have come."

She jerked up, holding her right hand to her stomach.

"The Fifth Brigade," Mlamuli stammered. "They are in the village."

"Go up to the attic!" she whispered, still drowsy and forgetting that the Gumede house had no hiding place like her father's house. Mlamuli didn't react to the command; he sat on the bed and held her hand. He was shivering and she patted him on the back, displaying a calm beyond her years. "They are looking for dissidents," she assured. "They will not harm us."

If only she were right.

Acting as if they were preparing to greet and welcome the soldiers, Mlamuli and Sarah walked to the parlor and sat on the couch by the entrance to his parents' bedroom. They hugged, said short prayers, held hands, and waited. Soon thereafter, a scratchy beep sounded in front of the house. Two gunshots rang. But Sarah and Mlamuli didn't leave the couch. Their breathing, though, grew louder and sweat seeped from their palms. A soldier burst into the house and shouted something in Shona and then in English. "Dissidents, surrender!"

Mlamuli and Sarah sprang up from the couch and stepped forward. Two more soldiers stomped inside the house and quickly spread out. They went into the rooms, overturning everything they could.

Staring at the two rather nastily, the first soldier asked, "Where is your father? Where are the dissidents?"

Collecting himself from the shock of the soldier's command, Mlamuli replied that there were no dissidents in their house.

"You're dissidents," another soldier shouted.

"We are not dissidents," Sarah said calmly.

"Shut up," the first soldier shouted. "Oh, look at you. You're pregnant. Who made you pregnant? You want to fill our country with dissidents."

The soldier pointed the bayonet affixed to the nozzle of his gun to the small bulge of Sarah's stomach. Mlamuli stepped forward and moved the nozzle away from her. The soldier chuckled and looked at Mlamuli so that their eyes met.

71

"An Ndebele warrior," he said and pointed the gun at his leg. "What ate your leg? An *ngozi*?"

The soldier chuckled to himself. "Where is your father?" he asked.

"He went to Antelope Mine to receive his pension," Mlamuli answered.

"You're a liar," the soldier shouted. "He is a dissident. You know where he is."

"You have to tell us where the dissidents are, tell us," one of the soldiers commanded.

"Have you ever supported them?" another asked.

"No sir. We support our prime minister. My father named me after him. My name is Robert."

The soldiers screeched a laugh. "Look at him! Robert! Ndebele Robert?"

"My mother was Shona," Sarah addressed the first one. "The dissidents took her."

"A liar," shouted the first soldier and tired of the fruitless interrogation, he commanded the other soldiers to take them both.

Sarah and Mlamuli joined about 30 villagers at one of the village squares. Most were elderly men and women, along with a few youths and children. A very tall soldier with a thin beard stepped forward and fired several bullets in the air for attention. "We know that you have been supporting the dissidents," he roared. "Tell us where they are. Otherwise, we will kill all of you! All of you!"

A man in his late seventies ambled forward. "We have no dissidents here," he said. "We don't know where they are."

"You're telling lies!" shouted the commander. "You're all liars, *hundi*! Tell us where they are hiding now."

"We support our prime minister," the man pleaded.

Children cried. So did some elderly women. Sarah leaned on Mlamuli for support and sobbed in his arms. He assured her that it all was just an empty threat. The soldiers knew that they were not dissidents and would soon leave them alone.

Irked by Sarah and Mlamuli's hugging, the soldier who earlier pointed his bayonet at Sarah's stomach went straight over to her and ordered her to walk to the front. At the same time, another soldier dragged another pregnant woman, whose stomach was much more pronounced than Sarah's, to the front of the crowd. Mlamuli trudged forward, rightly suspecting what the soldier had in mind. "Hey, cripple. Step back!" the soldier shouted, pointing his gun at him. Sarah stared at Mlamuli, urging him to comply and to remember his own words that all was merely a threat.

But it wasn't. God, it wasn't a threat.

Gnashing his teeth loudly, the soldier pointed his gun at Sarah's head and, without any further threat, pulled the trigger. A shot rang. A collective scream of shock swept the group. Then silence, as Sarah's body dropped to the ground. With the same unflinching ease, he turned to the other pregnant woman. He shot. Unsatisfied with the extent of his horror, he pulled out his bayonet and plunged it into her stomach. He yanked it through, from her chest down to her crotch. In seconds, her child was wriggling in his left hand. He picked it up and held it out to the villagers. A collective groan swept through the group. "Look here! This will happen to all of you if you don't take us to the dissidents," he said and let the child fall with a thud.

Mlamuli stood like a pillar, staring at Sarah's body and her pulsing blood, unbelievingly. Suddenly his knees caved and he slumped to the ground. In a gritty resolve, he crawled to Sarah, knowing full well the most likely consequences of his action. But it no longer mattered to him whether he was bayoneted or shot in the head. Alas, it no longer made any difference to him that he existed. Nor did it make any difference to the soldiers that he did. They had moved on, ignoring him and his Sarah. They had moved on with the group, herding them to where he didn't know.

Sihle

Yvonne fought back her emotion by coughing lightly. She was satisfied with the image of Mlamuli, regardless of how violent the scenes were to her. She glanced at her watch. She had to think through other characters, she thought, and, writing down the next name, Sihle, closed her eyes.

◆◆

Dr. Nandini Sen raised her head from a gaunt boy with ashy, dark skin and tumescent stomach, who followed her every movement with his large, empty eyes. She was happy with his condition. She checked the infusion hanging from the IV pole at the head of the bed, and wiped sweat from her forehead with the back of her hand.

Dr. Sen still had some more patients to attend to. Before that, however, she had to breathe some fresh air, so she walked to the side window overlooking the small space between the two shacks that were the camp's hospital. Retrieving a handkerchief from her pocket, she wiped off more sweat that trickled down her soft cheeks and longish neck. She could see many raggedly dressed soldiers clutching their AK-47s like children hold their toys. They were posted at different paths that led to approximately 20 largely decrepit I-shaped shacks that stood haphazardly in twos and threes, very much removed from the hospital.

Having had enough fresh air, she returned to her duty, walking to an aged and haggard woman who was humming a song to herself. As Dr. Sen stood by her bed, the woman looked up. "Did you hear any news from Kezi?" she asked in a phlegm-filled voice.

"Kezi?" Dr. Sen asked, struggling to hide her confusion.

The woman closed her eyes as though offended that Dr. Sen didn't understand her instantly and went on with her song. Then, reviving her interest in the doctor, she felt her apparel. Their eyes met and Dr. Sen smiled. The woman didn't smile back but kept her eyes on the doctor, who bent over her, then sat on the edge of the bed. She asked the woman for her name.

"My name is Mrs. Sihle Dumede," she said, batting her eyes in slow but determined succession. Dr. Sen noted the name, without removing her eyes from the patient.

"From Kezi, right?" Dr. Sen asked.

"Yes," Mrs. Gumede said. "Kezi is beautiful. My family is in Kezi. Please, don't leave me alone. Don't go away," she pleaded.

"I'm not going away," Dr. Sen assured.

"Please, save my life, doctor," Mrs. Gumede went on. "I want to see my husband and children."

"I'll save your life."

Mrs. Gumede smiled, closed her eyes, while Dr. Sen felt her pulse and listened to her heartbeat and lungs. She cast her eyes on the infusion container and moved on to the next patient, while her mind churned over the promise she had made.

Doctor Sen was among the few members of *Doctors Without Borders* who had been allowed to attend to the sick at Bhalagwe Camp. It was an effort by the Mugabe regime to show the world there was nothing like the mass executions that the BBC had claimed. Bhalagwe Camp, according to Mugabe, was nothing other than a factory. He allowed the humanitarian organization to visit on the condition that no reporter and no white person went along. So, the medical personnel consisted of two Indians, two Chinese and two Nigerians, one of whom nearly derailed the mission with her meltdown at seeing many withered people. *I was like this as a child! It's hunger! Hunger! I was a Biafran kid. I had kwashiorkor.* Luckily for her and the members of her team who literally held their breath all the time, none of the government escorts heard her outburst.

Thanks to the neutral report submitted by the organization that expressed gratitude to Mugabe for having allowed them to attend to the sick for seven consecutive days without intervention, the BBC news was not confirmed. In appreciation of their cooperation, Mugabe granted them their one plea: to transfer the patients to Mambali Clinic, near Botswana and far removed from the notorious Bhalagwe Camp. They could take better care of them there.

The heat at Mambali Clinic wasn't as intense as that at Bhalagwe. Dr. Sen, slender and pale, stood under a tall jacaranda tree beside one of the two buildings of the Clinic, chewing furiously at her gum. It was her first break of the day. She waved at a doctor, who went into one of the two emergency vans in front of the hospital.

After more than a week at the clinic, Nandini hadn't yet overcome the shock of finding that Sihle Gumede wasn't among the evacuees. What could have happened to her? Did she die? Was she still at Bhalagwe? None of the people she asked knew Sihle Gumede in person. They knew Kezi, though, and they confirmed to Dr. Sen that Gumede was a common name there. Indeed, one of the young men she asked promised he would take her to a woman from Kezi who also went by the name Gumede. It was he she waited for under the jacaranda tree. It didn't take much longer for his arrival.

They walked back to the hospital where he pointed at a sallow woman. "Here she is," he said. "She is from Kezi."

The woman looked up at Dr. Sen, who attempted a smile. Stepping closer, the doctor observed that the left part of the patient's upper lip had a gash so that it appeared she had a harelip. She greeted her and perched on the edge of the woman's bed. That seemed to have appealed to the sick woman, who smiled, exposing a gap at the gashed side of her lip. "How are you?" Dr. Sen asked.

"I'm doing well, doctor," came a crisp, lively voice. The answer surprised Dr. Sen, who remembered attending to this patient two days earlier and trying in vain to exchange words with her. The woman's much friendlier attitude this time around pleased her. Yet the woman went on in what was no less than a London middle-class accent: "I want to live, doctor," she said in a low tone of voice. "I'm dying to get back to life," she added, prompting a hearty smile from Dr. Sen, who enjoyed the play on words.

"I don't look good, do I?" the woman went on, placing her hand on her chest as though to draw the doctor's attention to that part of her body.

Dr. Sen stared intently at the woman's bandaged breasts and at her lip. "Who did this to you?" she whispered and quickly scanned her surroundings, knowing that she had broken an unspoken rule. Hadn't they promised Mugabe that they were there only to heal the sick and never to go beyond that? Indeed, Dr. Sen and others kept that promise all the while. But she obviously couldn't any longer. And no sooner had she uttered this taboo question than tears shone in her eyes.

"Will I make it out of here?" the woman asked. And when Dr. Sen didn't answer immediately, she went on to assure herself that she would make it. "I'll not die," she said more to herself. "This is not Bhalagwe."

"You're right. It's not," the doctor assured. "What is your name?" she asked, happy for what she believed would change the discussion a bit.

"I'm Zandile."

"Zandile?" the doctor pronounced nearly as flawlessly as the other had.

Zandile nodded. "You're the first non-Zimbabwean to get it right," she said. "Friends call me Dile."

The doctor went on to pronounce the name again in what she interpreted as pleasing to Dile. "I am Nandini. I was looking for a woman called Sihle Gumede."

"I know," Dile said. "I heard that. They said that a white woman was looking for somebody from Kezi."

"White woman. That's not me."

"They meant you. You're white."

"No, I'm Indian."

"Everyone on the lighter side of my fair skin is white for these people," Dile explained through a tight smile on her lips. She looked beautiful. And Dr. Sen told her.

"Ah, please," Dile said.

"I really mean it. You are."

Dile took a deep breath, doing her best to hide her pain. "I'd have come to you if you hadn't come with this question. I admire you so much."

"Why?"

"I understand you're part of a humanitarian organization. I'm not sure I'd have done that even if I'm paid like the American movie stars."

Dr. Sen smiled. "You're very funny," she said.

"I mean it. Sometimes I ask myself why you guys do all these things. Literally, you give your lives for people you don't know. Why do you do this?"

"I don't know. Growing up, I always felt the desire to connect with people. I thought it's what drove me to becoming a doctor. It was like hunger that wouldn't quit."

"And you have to endure all this? The stench, the cries, the awful sights."

"I didn't know that any doctor sees anything better. It's no different than in India."

"One is almost helpless in the face of all this, right?"

"The most one can do is to heal as much as one can."

"You sound like Dr. Rieux in Camus' *The Plague*."

"I don't know him. I've heard about that book, but I haven't read it."

"That was the last book I read in London before I came here."

"In London? You used to be in London?"

Dile closed her eyes and took a deep breath; she puckered her lips in regret. "It's a long and sad story. I'll tell you."

"Does your name have any significance?" Dr. Sen asked as though to demonstrate she wasn't too eager to get into Dile's misery. That in turn brought the two even closer.

"I was the fourth and the last of my mother's children. All girls. That's why I was given that name. Girls are enough," Dile chuckled. "That's the meaning. I bet it must have come from my father, who left us after my birth."

Dr. Sen was happy for Dile's humor. "I'm the only girl in my family of three children," she said.

"You must be lucky. They all will surely be proud of you."

Dr. Sen put on an indifferent smile. "They're not," she said flatly.

"I miss my family," Dile went on. "They are still in London. I used to go to school there. School of Oriental and African Studies. My mother and sisters warned me not to travel to Zimbabwe. There were troubles in the country. But we heard they were caused by Ndebele dissidents. I am Ndebele. But we were against the dissidents. We never understood why they would foment problems in the newly independent country. I should have known better. When I heard that Mugabe was after them, I didn't think I'd eventually be counted as one of them. So, I went to visit my grandma. That was the official reason, but my sisters knew why I made the journey. I wanted to spend time with my boyfriend, Charles Manyika, a writer, who had just gone back to Zimbabwe from London. It was while I was visiting him that the soldiers of the Fifth Brigade caught me.

"I left London on March 25, 1983, a week before Easter. Charles picked me up from the Harare International airport in the evening. As he held me in his arms, he announced in an unmistakably nervous voice that Mugabe had started an offensive against the dissidents in Matabeleland. I said that it was a good idea and that those scallywags needed to be stopped. But he wasn't entirely enthusiastic about my comment. He simply said that he was afraid of Mugabe because he knew him. I couldn't claim that I knew Mugabe. I have never seen him in person. Indeed, I have always thought of him as our liberator. I was one of the many who celebrated in London in April 1980, when we finally became a sovereign nation.

"We spent two days in Harare before traveling to Rusape, Charles's birthplace where his mother still lived with his two younger brothers. We spent three days there, after which we set off for Kezi to see my grandma. We shouldn't have taken that journey, you know. I should have taken people's fears more seriously.

"Not many in Manicaland knew exactly what was happening in Matabaleland. They were like two different worlds. One Shona, the other Ndebele. There were hints of some killings of innocent people in Tsholotsho but I, foolishly enough, thought it truly had to do with the killing of dissidents. I batted down Charles's doubts and we went on with our travel plans. On our way to Kezi, we encountered a group of red beret-wearing soldiers. They spoke Shona, to which Charles had no problem replying, being Shona himself. I spoke no word of Shona. Not even *I love you*. We said it in French."

She smiled self-effacingly. "Charles loved French like the Americans love their flags," she joked.

"It might have sounded weird to the soldiers that I didn't respond to whatever they were saying and one of them asked me a question to which I merely stared. Then he shouted that I was Ndebele. That offended Charles. He saw it as an insult that no less than three years after we had collectively fought the whites, we would make such differentiations. He barked that it was primitive to ask such a question; it was unfair and backward-looking. Perhaps he believed he would shout sense into them. That was a mistake. They beat him up. Right there in my presence. I quickly jumped in to intercede, but one of the soldiers gave me a brutal kick to my groin. The pain shot at the speed of lightning right to my heart and up to my brain. I fell down.

"Charles whispered that I should back off. I could be shot right there, I realized. I gave up. They tied up my hands and pushed me into a van. They left him lying by the side of the road. My most painful moment was seeing his eyes while I was being driven away. It was like the eye of an elephant on the man who had just fatally shot it. I felt guilty. I felt I had betrayed him.

"That was how I came to Bhalagwe Camp. I became a slave there. One of seven young women forced to live in the officers' building that was apart from the camp where the rest of the Ndebele people were held. Any officer could come to you any time he chose. You didn't allow him to ask for it. He would do it with the butt of his gun. He wouldn't stop beating you until he saw blood."

She pointed at her harelip, and the missing tooth. "The butt of a gun. It broke my resistance. Blood was everywhere. Yet he had me. Cursing me. Calling me names. Defiling me. I had at least two men every day. Or rather, two men had me." She paused, looked away.

"Then I became pregnant. But that didn't put them off. Quite the contrary. It seemed to excite them more. You had to make it possible for them, for their sadistic imagination. I prayed they didn't know when I would go into labor. One of us went into labor as two officers just arrived from their field operation. The girl's whining amused them. They tied her legs together and left her in their room. They locked it up and left."

"Goodness, like in Auschwitz?" cried Dr. Sen.

"I bet ours was worse," said Dile and went on with her story. "The girl cried the whole day. Then she stopped. When the soldiers returned the following day, they disposed of her body. I knew that the same fate awaited me. It would be logical. So, when the pain began, I did everything within my power to conceal it. I told Nkosi, one of us, who was in her third month. She encouraged me to

81

endure it till the last minute. I was lucky it came early in the morning. Around 4 AM. I awoke Nkosi. She accompanied me to the small bush in the back of the house. God, I was lucky. It didn't take much time. It didn't live."

She looked at Dr. Sen. "I didn't allow it to," she whispered.

Dr. Sen placed her hand on Dile's stomach in a gesture of solidarity.

"Although I never really got attached to the child, I felt as if an important part of me had just been sucked out. From that moment onward every place looked dark. At times I couldn't even raise my hand up to my chest. I felt angry toward everything. If only I had taken Charles's fears seriously. If only we just visited his mother and then went back to Harare which was heaven compared to what was going on in Kezi. I wanted to die. That was infinitely better than having to experience all this. I could no longer bear the chorus of cries coming from one particular shack that I later learned was a torture chamber. People cried like animals in a slaughterhouse. I could no longer bear hearing gunshots, knowing that the bullets were sinking into people's hearts. Their heads. Their stomachs. And they were your people. Those who spoke your language. Their crime: They weren't Shona."

She wiped her tears. "I'm sorry."

"Oh, please," Dr. Sen uttered.

"A few days later, one of the officers wanted to sleep with me. I was having intense pain down there. I refused. He unbuckled his belt and began to beat me. He targeted my breasts. I gave no resistance. I even yelled out that he should kill me. He didn't. The following day, I was transferred to the general people's camp. That was where I met Sihle Gumede."

The doctor looked up, lips pursed in an attempt to hold her emotion together.

"I came to know her when she was going out of her mind. She was humming a popular song I used to hear while growing up in Kezi. The song was about Kezi's beautiful hills. It was about the stone virgins drawn on the rock inside Gulati cave there. Gulati cave was the most sacred of places. A womb where fertility was renewed. I, too, loved everything about Kezi and its hills. I joined her in the song. We hummed together. Then her eyes misted with tears that flowed gently to her sunken cheeks. She looked piteously gaunt. Like most people, anyway.

"After our songs, she told me about her family. The soldiers caught her on the way. That was how she came to Bhalagwe Camp. She asked me if I could find her family and tell them about her. I promised her I would."

"And I promised her I'd save her," Dr. Sen said, fighting back tears.

"No, you couldn't have saved her," Dile said. "She had already lost it here," she added touching her forehead. "You couldn't have saved her," Dile repeated.

Dr. Sen clenched her left fist tightly, almost digging her nails into her flesh. Her tears trickled down to the lapels of her overcoat. She began to whisper words to calm herself. She stood up, patted Dile's left hand in a clear indication that she wanted to be alone. Their eyes met. Dile nodded.

Dumiso

Yvonne fought back tears, while trying to let go of the images of Sihle and Zandile. Yet some drops trickled. Did she reckon with the fact that an artist's creation could turn out to influence the artist? She hoped that at least this story would be an accurate microcosm of what took place in her homeland. Taking a deep breath, she underlined the next name, Dumiso.

◆◆

Maphisa was a small town characterized by its averageness. It was beautiful, though it did not compare to Kezi that lay 20 kilometers to the north. No, it did not, for Kezi was a serene and scenic town surrounded by hills and caves. Maphisa was tragic, though not as tragic as Bhalagwe Camp, a few kilometers to its left. Maphisa had never been important, except for its gold deposits that attracted the white people. And since Cecil Rhodes and his tradesmen couldn't pronounce its Ndebele name, they called it Antelope Mine.

Antelope Mine was not beautiful. No, it couldn't be beautiful, for it, too, was now a camp—a death camp. Those shacks where the African gold miners used to live, hardworking Shonas and Ndebeles and Zulus and Xhosas and many other people from all around, now harbored only Ndebeles. And they were not to dig out gold. They were to pay the ultimate price of simply being who they were.

They were not supposed to live. They were supposed to die. In fact, they were already dead in the minds of their Shona lords, just as the Jews were already dead in the minds of the SS soldiers. They only had to bide their time. While they awaited their fate, they dutifully helped to get rid of the dead. That was why Mlamuli was brought there. He, the figuratively dead, buried the truly dead.

Maphisa was a grave. With its many mining shafts reaching to the belly of the earth, it appeared to be insatiable, for whatever was thrown into it, it gulped with an accompanying echo of *more, more, and more*. With time, though, it

85

could no longer contain more bodies that were forced down its throat. It spewed them back through the over-flooded shafts. Oh, Maphisa, how harmless is your name! Antelope Mine, how heavenly you sound.

Shortly after his arrival in the camp, Mlamuli glanced at the pile of washed up bodies several meters from where they were digging graves. He saw the colors of a shirt and trousers on a particular body. He had seen that shirt and trousers before. But he couldn't be quite sure, for he viewed the bodies from afar. He knew he'd have more time to look closer when they carried the bodies into the grave. Sweat streamed down his forehead, his armpits, his neck—everywhere—as he, together with other men, young and old, dug into the piece of land that three of the red-beret-wearing soldiers chose. When he saw that the soldiers were not looking at them, he stepped closer to Joshua Moyo, a white-haired man in his mid-sixties, his newest friend from the evening before. "I think I saw my father there," he whispered.

"Among the dead?"

"I saw clothes that looked like the ones he wore the day he left home," he whispered.

"Hey there!" shouted a soldier, taking two steps in their direction. "Do your job and stop talking," he commanded. Luckily for the two, he stopped there and merely pointed his AK-47 at them. Using the butts of the guns on the captives wasn't rare.

Mlamuli bent down and dug on. But his mind didn't let go of what he glimpsed earlier. He still remembered when he brought that particular light-blue, short-sleeved shirt for his father before Dumiso set out for Antelope Mine.

Satisfied with the depth of the grave the captives dug, the soldiers commanded them to move on to the pile of bodies; some had decomposed, others were mainly bloated. The body Mlamuli had seen earlier was one of the bloated ones. His suspicion grew stronger when he stepped closer and saw the brown trousers. The formerly loose trousers were now tight on the legs and the shirt had burst its buttons.

He looked at Joshua, and stared intently at the body. Joshua looked back at him, his face contorted, as if the sight lit some spark. Did he recognize the body, too? At the same time, he saw that one of the soldiers was looking at them.

Joshua whispered to Mlamuli that they should bend down to work and called to one of the other captives to help them carry that body.

◆◆

"Your father was a good man," Joshua said to Mlamuli as they sat under a small marula tree, one of the many that dotted the front of the cluster of shacks where they lived. It was late evening and they could hardly see each other. It was one of the few evenings they didn't have to assemble to be lectured to by soldiers who never failed to remind them they were *hundis* for supporting the dissidents.

Life in the camp was no longer as brutal and as unbearable as it used to be, Joshua told his younger friend. A few months ago, when he was transferred there from Bhalagwe camp, the soldiers beat them nearly every day.

"I used to be stronger than I am now," he said. "Now, I am a shadow of myself. I am from Tsholotsho. I was a mechanic. I worked for Mr. Njabulo. I was in my office when the soldiers came. They accused me of making a phone call to my master who had fled to Bulawayo. The Fifth Brigade made it known that they wanted to kill him. They killed all rich men around, whether they were dissidents or not. That was why my master went to hide. So, I called him to let him know that the soldiers were still around.

"The first time they came to our shop, they asked, 'Where is Mr. Njabulo? Where is Mr. Njabulo?' I can never forget that day. I can never forget the hate in their eyes. They were pointing their guns everywhere, putting their eyes in every corner. When they did not find my master, they left. But they came back the following day. They came back for me. They put me in a Puma vehicle along with other men.

"They took us to Mbama Police Camp. It was about a one hour drive. Throughout the drive we did not exchange words. We were very afraid. The soldiers had their guns pointed at us and we knew they could easily shoot us. We had already seen them shoot people without cause.

"At the Police Camp, the soldiers beat us like we were snakes. One of them used a heavy stick on my teeth. Four of my teeth fell out immediately. The two other men had their hands and feet tied together. One was punished more than the other two of us were. They just tied him to a tree, head-down for many hours. Blood came out from his eyes and nose. God, how can people be without hearts?

"When they untied him, he could no longer speak, nor even react to anything. He moped around like a donkey. They shot him. They just shot him. They made the two of us dig his grave. The following day we were sent to Bhalagwe Camp where I spent two months. It was from Bhalagwe camp that I was transferred to this place. Since then I have been digging graves.

"Your father, arrived two days after me. I was nearby when they interrogated him. He explained that he did not fight during the liberation war and that he was not a dissident. But that did not help him. They said that if he did not fight in the liberation war, it meant he wasn't interested in the freedom of Zimbabwe. He was not part of *chimurenga* because he chose to serve the white man by working in the gold mine. So, he betrayed his fatherland. They beat him.

"Your father was a strong man. He fought for his life. Well, what could he do in the face of it all? They laughed at him when he told them that he supported Mugabe and that he named his son after Robert Mugabe because he admired the freedom fighter. Was it you he referred to? You're Robert?"

"Yes, it was me," Mlamuli said. "But I hate this name now. I don't want to be called Robert any longer."

"It is not your fault. It was also not your father's fault. We all thought we were on a good road to liberation. We all were happy. Well, I supported Nkomo. He was a distant relative of mine. So, you can understand why."

"He should have given me another name."

"I don't know whether it could have saved us. Well, he did his best. He died peacefully. He didn't suffer a lot."

"Did they beat him?"

"Yes, but that was not the cause of his death. He died of thirst," said Joshua. "He was always thirsty. He wanted to drink but the soldiers did not allow him to. I couldn't help him. I and two other men were commanded to carry his body to the mine shaft at the root of the hill, behind the three shacks that collapsed. That was where we threw him. That was where we threw many corpses. Those

88

brought from Bhalagwe Camp. Those brought from Kezi. Those brought from Plumtree. Donkwe-Donkwe. Mbuya. Ndebele's young men and women. Our people. The empty shafts ate them all. Our people."

"God!" Mlamuli blurted.

"Yes, God will have the last say."

Mlamuli kept silent.

"Don't you believe so?" Joshua asked.

"I don't know," he said and told his story. "I stopped thinking about God when I knelt over Sarah's body and it was not moving any more. I called her name. I shook her. Her body was still warm. I thought that she saw my eyes. I stopped thinking of God. God had nothing to do with it all. God was silent. He never answered.

"My sisters helped me bury Sarah in our backyard. They called on God. I did not. Nor did I cry. I couldn't. That was when I lost all fear of the soldiers. I no longer cared whether they caught me or not. But my sisters still feared. They feared that the soldiers would do to them what a dissident did to Sarah. Or worse. I feared for them. They loved me very much. You know, I was an adopted child, but they never made me feel that way."

"Dumiso never revealed you weren't his blood son," said Joshua.

"No one knew outside our family," Mlamuli went on. "We were one. Really like we were one blood. I promised my sisters I would go find mama. That was why I left for Antelope Mine. The soldiers caught me on the way. I thought they would ignore me the way they had once before because of my leg. But it was a mistake to think so.

"It was on the Kezi-Bulawayo road that they caught me. Our bus was about to leave the asphalted road and to head toward Maphisa when two soldiers emerged from the nearby bush. They directed the bus to Bhalagwe. We arrived at Bhalagwe at the time their commander was addressing a group of people, so we were forced to join them.

"The commander said that his name was Jesus and that he was one of the leaders of *Gukurahundi*. He said he had gallons of blood in his car. He said that he was a vampire and he fed only on blood. His life was to drink the enemy's blood and that his supply was running low. So he came to this place to fill it up.

"After his speech, they divided us into four groups: boys, men, girls, and women. That evening they called me out with four other young men. Two soldiers began to beat me with sticks. They were laughing. Laughing at my jerks and cries of pain. They were saying, 'Look at the cripple. Look at that. He feels pain.'

"They used the field electric telephone, the one that works on battery power. Wires were tied to my penis and then they wound the machine the way women do on sewing machines. The shock ran through the body and I screamed. It threw me down but I could not remove the wires because I was handcuffed. They said, 'Oh, his penis is not like his leg. Look at Lobengula penis.' I wanted to die. I wanted them to just shoot me.

"The following day my genitals were swollen. But they healed weeks later. Then I began to dig graves. I dug graves every day. They took us to different places. We dug all morning. We threw dead people into those graves. We covered them. After a while, we stopped digging graves because sometimes we dug up bones. That was when they brought us to this place. Because Bhalagwe is a grave.

The Stone Virgins

Yvonne looked around and saw that people were trickling back to the hall. She took a deep breath and smiled to herself, admiring the work of the Muses. How on earth did they give her Nandini Sen whom she met in Toronto in her second year of study? Both remained friends until Yvonne's death. She sighed with regret as she ran back through the story of how Nandini came to learn Sihle's fate. *Oh, poor Sihle,* she thought. *Who knows where her remains were dumped?*

Yvonne was somewhat confident about what she would tell. She thought that with the help of these supporting stories she might as well just narrate those of the sisters exactly as she did in *The Stone Virgins*. Her heart began to pound and she thought she should pick out a few sentences from the book as a mnemonic device. And so, she took up her book and began to page through it, memorizing important scenes and expressions and words and images that would help anchor the sisters' story.

She kept the book aside and stared ahead for a while, making certain not to blink, lest her tears flow. That was exactly what she didn't need; she made up her mind: she would go up and just tell whatever came to mind, regardless of the order. She would open her mouth and Zimbabwe would speak. She simply had to tell stories like the others before her had done, like it had always been done in Africa, from time immemorial.

◆◆

Olaudah Equiano welcomed all back to the trial and announced that it was time to hear *Gukuranhundi* stories. He apologized that it was impossible to invite any of those who died during that time. In their place, however, Yvonne would step up to the podium and tell parts of their stories. If, after that, there was still need for more, they would be invited. He extended his right hand to Yvonne and gently motioned her to come forward.

Yvonne managed a smile despite her nervousness as she walked to the spot the other storytellers had occupied. She bowed to the judges, to Mugabe, and to Nkomo and the other dignitaries with him. Looking at the audience, her eyes meeting with the many thousands of people, all of whom eagerly returned her gaze and whose ears all yearned to hear her stories, she attempted to clear her throat in the old village storytelling fashion, but no sound came forth.

"Go on, sister," a male voice said. "We are here for you."

"Thank you," Yvonne said. She needed that encouragement. She glanced at her notebook and read a title to herself: Mlamuli Robert Gumede. "This is about the two pregnant young women in Cewale, who were disemboweled by the soldiers of the Fifth Brigade," she said.

A gasp of shock ran through the hall, trailed immediately by an equally stunned silence while Yvonne told them about the young women from Mlamuli's perspective. Before she even reached the brutal disemboweling of the two young women, many people were wiping tears. Some of them whispered, "Tell us no more, tell us no more. You are breaking our hearts."

But she went on, satisfied that she had struck a nerve, satisfied that she was rendering the people's stories as honestly as they happened. She glanced again at her notebook and announced, "This is the story of Sihle, who went in search of her husband. Sihle died wretchedly." And looking up to Dambudzo Marechera, said with pride in her voice, "Sihle died in the house of hunger."

He nodded. They both understood. But, apparently, they were not the only ones to understand. Some one had also read Marechera's book and his voice rang out a memorable line from it: *strange irruptions of a disturbed universe*, to which some people applauded. Mugabe apparently knew the line. He did not look up, for he feared meeting Marechera's eye.

Yvonne rendered the stories more perfectly than she had initially conceived them. She was happy. Not wanting to leave the people without some elements of hope, she told how Cephas Dube, Thenji's boyfriend, united with Nonce and offered her his friendship, devoid of carnal desire. A man loving a woman without carnal interest! That, indeed, was the dawn of a new age in Africa. When she was done, the people were torn between applauding or crying, between hope and despair, between hatred and love.

Not so for a thin, elderly woman who stood when Yvonne returned to her pew. With the help of a stick, the woman walked straight up to the judges and knocked on their table for their attention. She spoke to the judges in a voice hardly audible, even to the people seated in the front. "I cannot tell my story," she said. "But I want the world to hear it. I want you all to hear it. I have no voice. But my granddaughter has."

She turned to Yvonne. "Turn on that thing you showed before recess," she pleaded.

"What?" Yvonne asked. "YouTube?"

"Whatever you call it. My granddaughter is there. I know."

"What is her name?" Marechera asked.

"Bongani. Her name is Bongani. And my name? I am Maria Goretti Ncube."

In response to an encouraging nod from the chief judge, Yvonne turned to her keyboard and typed in the names. A white screen rolled down just in front of the judges: A slender woman doctor stands beside a bed and adjusts the infusion hanging on an IV pole. A skinny girl in her preteen is asleep. She seems to be having a bad dream and she turns and tosses without opening her eyes. She is saying something and she snaps at the air like a fish on a line. The doctor sits on her bed and places her hand on the girl's chest. She awakes. "Where am I?" she asks.

"You are in a hospital."

"Will I die?"

"No. I will save you. But you need to rest. Sleep."

"No, I don't want to sleep. Where is Grandma?"

"Your grandma?"

"Oh, the soldiers. They are bad, aren't they? They killed everybody."

"You will tell me about them, will you? You will tell me about your grandma, but sleep now."

Bongani is sitting on her bed. Beside her is the lean doctor, listening: "My name is Bongani. I am 12 years old. This is how Grandma died. She started dying on a Sunday. Her last seven days were bad. From Sunday to Sunday. First Sunday: I went to church. I returned. The sun was shining. Grandma sat in front of our house waiting for me. She was sleeping in her very old chair that she inherited from a white priest whose garden she took care of in Bulawayo many, many years ago. Her rosary has fallen from her hand. I woke her up. 'Grandma,

Grandma,' I called. 'I'm back.'

"She looked up with glassy eyes. The sun was on her face. It took her a while to recognize me. I said, 'It is me, Bongani.'

"'Ah, Bongani, my dear,' she said and extended her hand to me. I helped her move away from the sun into shade. I brought out four bottles of water and opened one for her. 'It is from the church,' I said. 'The priest brought some people to the church today.'

"'White people?' she asked.

"'Yes, a white man, a white woman, and two black women. They are from America,' I said.

"She drank and said, '*Aaaahh.* Holy water.'

"'No, it is not holy water,' I replied. 'They said it is vitamin water.'

"I explained that the people brought some food but dissidents stopped them and took it.

"My knees shook and my stomach talked. I thought I was about to fall. But I caught myself. I had to show Grandma that I was strong and that I haven't lost faith. She always told me not to lose faith. 'If you lose faith, you lose everything. There will always be water at Victoria Falls.'

"I told Grandma that the priest asked us to pray for the prime minister so that God would touch his heart and allow the food that the people sent to get to us. Grandma shook her head and said, 'That man is like the Pharaoh. But God will soon show him.'

"Grandma went on with her story about the white missionaries she served. 'They were good to me. Things were good until that man began to rule us. That man. He has the heart of stone.'

"I'm always surprised that even white people bring us food. Our teachers in the primary school said they were evil because they colonized our land and enslaved our ancestors. But I liked the white nuns. One of them once placed her hand on my head and called me her daughter. That was four years ago. We all went to church: me, Papa, Mama, Sibaso, and Grandma. That was before our troubles began, before Robert Mugabe became our prime minister, before the dissidents went everywhere causing confusion.

"I walked into our house and turned on the radio. I wanted to know whether the government has allowed relief food to come to Kezi. The batteries were weak so I heard only *shiiiiii, tok, tok, tok. Shiiiiii*. I removed them and placed them in the sun to recharge. There was nothing in the house—nothing. I didn't go to my parents' room. I was afraid of going there. I didn't want to see their wedding photo. Instead, I went to my room and sat on my bed. I felt like sleeping, but I told myself I shouldn't sleep. *Don't sleep, don't sleep, don't sleep.* I stood up and walked out to the front yard. Grandma was humming a song. I thought I saw some tears in her eyes.

"I was hungry. Grandma was hungry too, I knew. She never said so, but I knew she was. I took a deep breath and we looked at each other. I knew I had to go into the jungle, like I did three days ago when I killed a big rat and Grandma danced in her chair and sang and said I was the strongest girl she ever saw.

"The jungle was not as hot as the village. But it was very dangerous. Poisonous snakes, leopards, hyenas, and soldiers of the Fifth Brigade. A month ago a friend of mine stepped on a mine. It cut her two legs and she bled to death. But I was careful.

"I knew how to hunt. Sibaso taught me to hunt rabbits and squirrels. We were like twins even though he was older than me. He taught me a lot of things, like how to make stone slings that could throw stones very far away. He was good at firing stones at birds. He hardly missed. I miss him.

"The jungle was empty. No humans. No animals. Only the birds that chirped in the distance. Up in the topmost of trees. I've often climbed those trees in search of eggs. I never found them in their nests. Perhaps other hunters were faster than me. I wandered through the jungle, putting my eyes on every corner in search of wild fruits that I knew weren't there.

"After a while in the jungle I felt dizzy. I knew I had to get back home; otherwise, I would fall down. Just as I was about to step on the path that led to my village, I saw two lizards attached to one another at the waist. They could neither crawl together in one direction nor go their different ways. I picked up a stick and struck them. They became mine.

◆◆

"The next day. The sky was covered with some clouds and Grandma said it might rain. I hoped it did. After a while, she said we should pray. That was what the sky needed at the time. 'God works miracles,' she said. I knelt by her side and we prayed for rain, just as we have done for the last months. I believed in God. I believed in miracles. But I wanted to see one. Nothing that I prayed for has ever happened.

"While we prayed I looked at her skin. It was folded many times, like the neck of a turkey. I could see all her veins. I could see even her bones. I pitied her as we prayed. Not long after our prayers, the sun came out. The sun was as hungry as we were.

"We had no water. I had got to go fetch water from our river which was getting dry and dirty. It was a long distance, but I had to go. When I returned from the river, Grandma was asleep. I woke her and gave her water to drink. I was tired. My head hurt inside. My feet hurt. I went into the house. Again I didn't go to my parents' room because I didn't want to think about them. But as I lay in our couch, I couldn't sleep and I thought about them anyway. I saw them: I was in the bush hiding with other boys and girls. A soldier flogged Papa and shouted. Papa picked up a shovel and dug. Other men of the village also dug. They were nine. The soldiers were flogging him. Six women were singing but Mama was not among them. They sang: 'Mugabe is our leader. Mugabe is our liberator. Mugabe, Mugabe, Mugabe. Long live Mugabe. Long live Zimbabwe.'

"Papa and the other men finished digging. The soldiers told them to stand beside the ditch. They stood. The women were still singing. A soldier shouted, 'Stop!' The women stopped. Two soldiers stepped forward with guns in their hands. Papa looked around. I saw his eyes. I thought he saw me. The two soldiers pointed their guns at Papa and the other men. I heard some noise. Papa fell. Other men fell. They all fell into the ditch like logs of wood. The soldiers commanded the women to cover the grave.

"I didn't cry. My eyes refused to blink. I wasn't sure I was breathing. I thought I was in a dream. The three girls and a boy hiding with me in the bush didn't

96

cry. We were all shivering. The women filled in the ditch. The soldiers led them away.

"We came out from the bush very late in the evening. I met Mama and Sibaso. They said they saw what happened. Mama's eyes were full of tears and she couldn't speak. She hugged me. And she hugged Sibaso and Grandma. She said that we should pray for the souls of the dead and for our country. As we prayed, we heard some bangs on the door. Bang, bang, bang! 'Open the door!'

"Mama said, 'They are here! Sibaso, hide under the bed.' Sibaso didn't move. I pushed him, but he didn't react. The soldiers broke the door. One of them looked at Sibaso and said, 'Ah, look, a dissident!' Mama told him that Sibaso was not a dissident. 'He is my son. He is only 13 years old.'

"Grandma begged them, 'Please, please have mercy. Remember God!'

"They pushed her aside. But she continued to beg them and said. 'Remember, God sees everything.'

"'He's an Ndebele man,' one of the soldiers said.

"'He's not a man,' Mama said. 'He's a boy.'

"'He'll be a dissident,' the soldier said.

"I begged them, 'Leave my mama! Leave my mama!' One of them said to me, 'little girl, shut up.'

"The soldiers took Sibaso and Mama. Sibaso didn't cry. Mama didn't cry. She looked back at me and said, 'Bongani, take care of Grandma!' Grandma cried. I didn't. I went outside and sat down. I looked in the dark and refused to close my eyes. Sibaso never came back. I still hear Mama's last words. I would take care of Grandma. I would never allow her to die."

◆◆

"The next day. I went to our store to check whether I could find anything there—maybe a small bag of maize meal, some packets of biscuit, or a can of something. I found nothing and it made me feel ashamed. I drank some water, enough water to make my stomach feel full. An idea entered my head. I should somehow get into other people's houses and see whether I could find something there. But I knew the consequences if I were caught. People would shout that

I was a thief. I went anyway. I entered some houses that were no longer inhabited. I found nothing. But then I remembered that I had entered those houses before with some boys and girls. But you never knew. I went to what used to be stores. Still nothing.

"I walked into the bush and searched and searched and searched for anything. I saw an anthill. It was like a miracle. I was happy and I prayed, 'God let there be termites there.' I ran back home to get a hoe. Grandma advised me to be careful. Wherever there were termites, there were also reptiles that hunted them and snakes that hunted other reptiles. I took the hoe and met Stella on the way. She had a kind of fishing basket attached to a long stick with which she caught grasshoppers. She had already caught many and her Coca-Cola bottle was full. I asked her to join me in digging the anthill.

"There were many termites. Millions. I filled my empty *bournvita* can. I was happy. There were still many termites uncollected. Stella ran back home and got a container and filled it up."

◆◆

"We ate the second part of yesterday's termite catch for breakfast and drank plenty of water. Grandma smiled and sang, 'My Lord is my Shepherd. There's nothing I shall want.' When she was done with her song, she told me to turn on our radio.

"Since recharging the batteries last Sunday, I had turned it on only three times and then gave up. Each time, Robert Mugabe was speaking. He always had some warnings for us. Watch out for white people! White people were bad. They came from South Africa and America. They came from Britain. They planned to take back Zimbabwe. Then he swore we shall never be a colony again. These words weren't what I wanted to hear.

"Anyway, I obeyed Grandma and turned on the radio. I didn't like the song that was playing. After a while, we heard the news. Mugabe announced that operation *Gukurahundi* was succeeding. Soon, the whole country would be without dissidents because his soldiers were at work. I felt some pain in my chest and in my throat. I couldn't breathe normally. I looked at Grandma. She didn't look back at me. She was gnashing her teeth. She told me to turn off the radio. I turned it off and she took a deep breath and began to recite her rosary. I didn't join her. I was not sure whether I could ask God for anything at all because my heart was full of vengeance. I wanted Mugabe to die."

◆◆

"I went back to my anthill the next day. But I saw no termites there. Someone had dug deeper than I did. I walked around in search of another anthill. Many others have been dug into. I abandoned the search and went for squirrels. Luckily I found one. I aimed my stone sling at it. It was dead. I was happy. Something miraculous happened. Grandma stood up on her own after our meal.

"Sometimes I heard Sibaso's voice. Sometimes I thought that I saw my mother walking home with him. I missed them. I wanted her to be around so that I could cry. I just felt like crying.

"I missed my school. For three years now, no one talked about schools. Only the church was important. Sometimes I wished to go to church every day or every other day. The church was the only place we could meet other people. It was the only place we learned anything. God bless the priests and sisters who organized us. God bless them for telling us not to give up. They told us that the world has not forgotten us and we rejoiced.

"Sometimes, children cried. I told them that things would be all right. But after saying that, when they have stopped crying, I felt my eyes itch. I wanted to be alone."

◆◆

"The next day. I didn't want to get out of bed, but I could no longer sleep. Light came through the window cracks. I hated it. I heard my mother: *Bongani! What are you still doing in bed? Don't be lazy, Bongani! An idle mind is the devil's workshop.* I knew my mother was not in that room. But I wanted her to be. I wanted somebody to reproach me now.

"I waited. I waited for something to happen. But I knew nothing would ever happen. If I didn't put my legs out from the bed and make my feet touch the floor, they would not obey. This was what Mama always said. 'If you don't move your fingers, nothing moves. If you don't move your legs, nothing moves. If you don't do your homework, it won't get done.' But I waited.

"Then suddenly I thought I heard Grandma whisper my name. God, I've got to do something. I finally got out of bed and ran to her room. She was lying on her back, rosary in hand. Her mouth was slightly open. I greeted her. She greeted me in return. I helped her stand up and walked her to her chair. I told her that I was going to look for something. She nodded her head faintly as if she were not interested in whether I got something or not."

♦♦

"Sunday! Grandma was all cheers. I helped her sit in her chair and she sang me a song before I left for the church. It was her favorite song: 'Nearer my God to Thee, nearer to Thee.' Her voice was very weak and it quivered. I was sad and I told her not to sing that again. She told me to greet Father McGreevy for her. 'Tell him that it is Maria Gorretti Ncube. Tell him it is Maria the planter of fruited pumpkin.'

"I promised her I would greet him for her.

"There were some trucks in front of our church. A black priest was celebrating the mass. There were two white women, a black man, a black woman and a white man in the church. All but one woman looked old. They had wrinkles on their faces and looked like they were as old as Mama. The young one had blue eyes and small lips. Each time she looked at us, she smiled. Indeed, all of them seemed to be smiling except one of the men. He had a white beard. I couldn't take my eyes off them. I would tell Grandma what I was seeing and she would smile and remember her good old times in Bulawayo.

"I didn't know what the gospel was, or what the priest was preaching. I was thinking of what could be in the trucks. I was praying, 'God, let there be some food there!' I was tired of wandering in the bush in search of something. One of the white people addressed us during the mass. It was the young woman with blue eyes and small lips. She spoke slowly and told us that the whole world was praying for us. I liked her. I felt like going up there to hold her hands. She said that they have brought us food. Not much because they were not allowed to bring more. My heart jumped up and down in my chest like a tennis ball. I thought of Grandma. Oh, she should be here to hear these words.

"After the mass they gave us some packets of shortbread and bottled water. I got two packets. I tore one open and took out a piece. I put it between my teeth. Something tickled my salivary glands. My teeth sank into it like a sharp knife. It appeared to be what they had been waiting for.

"Saliva rushed to my mouth. I tasted many flavors in the bread. Some salt. Some sugar. I crushed something like a nut. Peanut? And then something like meat. And then something that felt like—I don't know. What I knew was that after four, five and six bites, the chunk in my mouth expanded. God! I've never eaten anything like that before. It performed magic in my mouth. The more I chewed the more it grew. It absorbed all my saliva. Just like the blotter we used to clean ink from our paper when we used to go to school. Then I opened a bottle of water and took a sip. The bread was happy to have that water and my mouth was full. I drank water again and again and again.

"Many people were eating theirs. Everyone was smiling. I finished two pieces and noticed sweat on the ridge of my nose and on my forehead. My stomach became big. I touched it and heard some sound inside. I went to the people and told them about Grandma. They didn't know Father McGreevy. I got some bottles of water and two packets of bread for her anyway. I thanked them and thought that Grandma would dance like a small girl.

"I came back from the church. Grandma was sitting in her chair in front of the house. I was happy that I would surprise her with gifts from the church. I walked to her. She was looking down to her navel. I greeted her but she didn't look up. I called, 'Grandma, Grandma.' But she didn't respond. She was still looking at a place. I touched her and then shook her. There was no response. Then her body leaned to one side. She fell. She lay on the spot where she fell, just the way she was sitting. She didn't breathe. I called her again, but there was no response. Then I got some headache. Then I heard some bees in my head. Then I saw some stars inside my eyes. My eyes were warm. I knew I was going to cry, but I didn't want to cry. I was just tired. All I wanted to do was sleep. Just sleep. So, I walked inside my room and climbed up my bed and slept.

Footnote #5

"And I? Where is my heart in all of this?"
J. M. Coetzee, *Age of Iron*.

The Verdict

When they finished watching the YouTube film, Maria Goretti Ncube wordlessly, reproachfully wagged her stick three times at Mugabe. She turned and trudged back to her pew without looking to meet the eyes of many who wanted to sympathize with her. People were murmuring curses to Mugabe.

Olaudah Equiano stood up, calmed down the audience and then informed all that the verdict would follow soon. To arrive at a just verdict, however, they needed to hear from the accused himself, so he told Mugabe that he would now have time to rebut all the stories and accusations he had heard. Mugabe was more than glad to do so; he immediately stood up and raised his voice loud enough for everyone to hear. "I have a question: Why am I standing trial?"

There was utmost silence as all eyes turned to him challengingly. Was he mad, stupid, or what? He was not disturbed by the shocked silence, though, and went on to justify his question. "Am I standing trial because I challenged Western imperialism? Could I have fought the West without some people dying? Why aren't you putting the real war criminals on trial?"

Emboldened by the stunned silence at his words, he went on in the same oratorical cadence: "Who among you can contest that white people stole our land? Who? Have they been put on trial? Carl Peters and the Germans had the first holocaust in Namibia; they exterminated the Hereroes. Did anyone care to ask about the Hereroes? Ian Smith killed more than 50,000 Africans. If those victims were Europeans, he would be dragged to The Hague. Wouldn't he? Piet Botha killed uncountable blacks in South Africa. Why isn't he in The Hague?"

"What, then, have you learned from the European man?" a man's voice asked.

That voice shocked Mugabe into silence for some seconds. But he shot back: "Nothing good can ever come from the European man!"

The man's question undoubtedly broke the dam of doubts that had piled on while Mugabe addressed the people. Another voice rose. It was a woman sitting in the second pew: "Were the white people all evil, all the time? Nothing to learn from them?" she asked.

Mugabe stared. He did not answer.

"So you learned nothing from the European man other than to kill your people?" another voice followed.

"I wasn't killing them. I was protecting them from the white predators. Our people have nothing in common with white people."

"Aren't you too sure of your opinion?" Yvonne asked.

"I know what I am talking about, woman. Black is black and white is white. Never in the world shall the two be one."

Some people began to murmur in disapproval. Equiano knocked his gavel three times for order. He turned to Mugabe. "Have you anything more to say?"

"I am here to tell you that imperialism never died. It is still alive, breathing in African kitchens. Imperialism goes to bed with every African. It wakes up with him. It must be stopped. The West is the root of Africa's problems. Great Britain. The United States. Those Europeans and their brothers and sisters in Africa. It is racism. Racism is the root of Africa's problems. Racism is the cause of all this. Racism! Neocolonialism! Neo-imperialism! If any African fails to understand this, he is a traitor to his people. He has turned his back on his ancestors. He has rejected the sufferings of his people. That is all I want to say. That's all I have to say."

When Mugabe finished his well-rehearsed rant-defense, Equiano announced that the three judges had to confer with the Almighty for the verdict. So they left. Their profiles were visible through the thin curtain as they approached the throne. It was very quiet in the hall, so quiet that people heard each other's breathing. In less than 10 minutes, the judges came back. Equiano announced that they had the verdict. He turned to Mugabe: "The Almighty recognizes what you have done for your people. The Almighty acknowledges that you and your people have suffered terribly at the hands of white people. But the Almighty also knows that your people have suffered terribly at your own hands. That was not what you all fought for. That was not what your people deserved. Remember, the Almighty also chose many others to bring about the progress of your people. You stood in their way. You became a stumbling block in your people's road to happiness. You have been found guilty on many counts. The Almighty has condemned you."

But Mugabe would have none of it. "How could this be?" he shouted. "How could I be condemned after all I did for my people? I liberated them from the hands of the white people. I helped them fight imperialism and neocolonialism and globalization and exploitation and capitalism and…"

Equiano hit his gavel on the desk to put a period to Mugabe's litany. "We have heard this already," he said.

Some people chuckled.

"But there is no evidence against me," he insisted.

"No evidence?" some voices asked in shock.

Equiano did not respond. Rather he turned to Steve Biko and gave him a slight nod.

"We did not condemn you," Biko said, standing up to address Mugabe. "The Almighty did. Besides that, however, there is ample evidence to condemn you. Each of the stories we have heard here is enough to send you to eternal hell fire, but the Almighty has looked down with mercy on you. The Almighty is not hardhearted. Your punishment has been softened. You will not be condemned to many years in hell."

Mugabe smiled. And just as he did, many voices yelled: "No, no, he belongs to hell. No other place is good for him."

Equiano raised his hand. "Quiet, people. This is God's verdict."

Biko went on with his address. "The Almighty chose to punish you for one of the many crimes," he said to Mugabe. "It is the crime of living in the past. You chose to live in the past."

"Stuck in the past," added Equiano.

"Selectively in the past," Marechera concurred.

"That is your crime. From this follow all others," Biko went on.

Agreeing that the Almighty's decision will be good enough for them, the people clapped in applause. Excited about the nature of the atonement that God chose for Mugabe, they chanted: *Punishment! Punishment! Punishment.*

"If I am not going to be condemned to hell, what then is my punishment?" Mugabe asked, some faint smile on his face.

"You must go back to earth. It is an opportunity for you to grow," Biko said.

"To grow?" Mugabe yelled. "What is that supposed to mean? I am 84 years old. I am an African elder. It is an insult to suggest that I am not grown."

"It is not an insult, my dear," Biko said. "That is the verdict," he added.

"I don't understand," Mugabe insisted.

"Do you really want to understand?" Biko asked.

Mugabe said nothing.

Biko turned to Marechera and nodded knowingly.

Marechera stood up, expressed his gratitude for the job for which he thought he was suited since he, too, was a Zimbabwean under Mugabe. He, too, was a typical postcolonial subject who had had some scuffles with whites. He then turned to Mugabe, ready to deliver what he, as in his former worldly self, would have called the *hermeneutical circle of dictatorship and poverty in Africa*.

"How could I interpret the verdict of the Almighty for you, your excellency? Where do I begin? How could I explain that you are not grown? I try my best to play the Hermes to you, sir, for though you used to fly on the wings of angels, you are now weighed down by your feet of clay and heart of stone. How do I begin to teach you, sir; you, who used to be my lord and teacher? I feel with you as much as my heart can go. But my feelings have nothing to do with the verdict of the Almighty. I feel with you, for in truth, you weren't always all evil. No, I cannot forget your contribution to our history. But the greater and more wide-ranging truth, the truth with existential implication, sir, is that having barely survived Ian Smith's torture chamber, your mind and soul became fixated on one singular goal: to avenge yourself on the white man. But should you be blamed for that? Should you be blamed for being angry and bitter? That's beyond my judgment. What I do know, sir, is that this singular passion for vengeance took possession of your being; it became the reason you lived for, your driving force for governance."

Marechera paused for effect, looked around, happy that people listened attentively. Then he went on. "Your excellency. It was not the desire to advance the well-being of your people that brought you to power; it was not the desire to aid the flourishing of life. No, it was retribution. Raw, animal retribution. In that respect, sir, you had the memory of an elephant. Like an elephant, though, you are imprisoned in your bulky animality. Should I tell you that retribution, sir, is antithetical to civilization; that it has no place in civil society? Should I tell you, sir, that the greatness of a leader is not measured on the degree of his

106

anger toward other people, it is not based on what he hated and destroyed, but on what he has built? It is based on how far he has enhanced the lives of his people. Should I tell you that, sir? I thought you knew. I thought you really loved Zimbabweans. I thought you wanted to expand space for our dreams. Unfortunately though, trees stopped to grow the day you became a powerful man.

"Frothing in your frenzy of vengeance, you became the archetypical African freedom fighter, who believed to have wrenched the torch of civilization from the gods for his people who, he thought, brooded in total darkness. You proclaimed yourself Prometheus. But in order that your torch might shine bright, you squelched your people's candles. Sir, you brooked no other light beside yours. You were lost in delusions of grandeur because your people wallowed in misery and fear. Is that greatness?

"We all fought the colonial master. We all wanted to defeat the enemy. And I? Where is my heart in all this? If only we had paused to ask this question. But we did not. And so we, we traded our souls to the devil in the belief it would help us defeat of our enemies. The enemies are gone. Where are our souls?

"If only you had allowed even a single, nameable idea to enter your world. Ach, if only you had been guided by something immortal, something that would go beyond your narrow village world. If only you had allowed a simple, but powerful act of forgiveness to guide your thinking for a while, white people who, both of us agreed, brought violence on us, could have learned something from you.

"Forgiveness, reconciliation! For the simple-minded ones, it is foolish, but for the wise it is deep. It strengthens the heart and puts the mind on the path of the good. White people could have learned from us."

He took a deep breath. "We, too, have a lot to learn from them," he added. "Do you remember our people's proverb? *A new thing does not come to she who sits, but to she who travels.* That is the wisdom of our ancestors. Ach, your excellency, what a palette of opportunities you missed. If only you had time to remember that leaders must have conscience. The moment they take on the scepter of power, the moment they take on that symbol, they no longer live just for themselves. They adopt the conscience of the world. It is saying yes to the heaviest of weights. The conscience of leaders separates them from the rest of us."

Marechera looked around, appearing surprised by the extent of his speech. "Goodness, what am I saying? I am getting carried away by a priestly instinct to preach. Sermons, I know, do not belong in courts of law."

He turned to Mugabe. "Believe me, sir, I am not a priest. I am a poet, a creator of words, a carrier of the calabash of wisdom. But I am also a historian. It is in my power as a historian that I try to locate the origin of your ailment so that you will be able to recognize where the real issues lie. Reminiscence! That is the word. And when you remember, you'll be able to warn others of the destructive powers of bitterness and lust for vengeance. Reminiscence, that is the word, because, as some thinkers would say, those who fail to learn from the past are bound to repeat its mistakes.

"Your excellency, sir. The Almighty looked upon you with mercy because you contracted a disease the moment Zimbabwe ceased to be a British colony. You remember the independence party in Government House in Harare?"

Humiliated with this remembrance, Mugabe nodded. "Yes, I remember, but every person was healthy and happy," he remarked.

"Yes, they were," Marechera said. "And that is why your failure is all the more painful. Oh, well, your excellency, I grant myself the permission to quote from Yvonne's book, from which she has read us stories. It goes thus: 'Naked hips danced Jerusalem dances at the small city hall for the first black mayor.' Yes, that was how happy we were when we began to rule ourselves. Naked hips. Supple hips. Innocent hips that did not realize we would soon be forced into a house of hunger.

"It was during these festivities, at the independence party, that you breathed in *viridae postcolonitis*."

"*Viridae postcolonitis?*" Mugabe exclaimed. "What is that?"

"Postcolonial virus, your excellency. Some kind of inflammation. But you did not know you had breathed in those dangerous viruses and they attacked your pituitary gland so that you no longer produced growth hormone. Within a year or so, you developed a full-blown postcolonial fever. You became developmentally delayed."

"Postcolonial fever?" asked Mugabe.

"Yes. And difficult to cure. You failed to mature, your excellency."

"Do I look immature?"

"Your bitterness neutered your antibodies and you did not realize your full potential. So, it turned out that you are like Kurtz, that white man in the tropics driven to insanity by absolute power and isolation. You remember? He was driven to lunacy by the utter weakness of the natives. You experienced extreme isolation because you sequestered yourself in your Manichaean understanding of the world as strictly shaped by white and black, good and evil, colonizer and colonized. You forgot that the world is larger than these binaries and that your people needed to have good living conditions. A good life is neither white nor black."

Visibly happy with his words, Marechera turned to Biko and nodded.

Biko stood up and said: "That is the reason the Almighty looked with mercy on your situation and wanted you to go back and start all over again. You stopped growing when you became all-powerful.

"It is an insult to the African dignity to imply that the colonizer was the impulse for our growth," Mugabe argued.

"No," said Biko. "I see it this way. When you were still colonized, you had a mission. You fought for freedom. That was a value worth dying for. But the moment you became free, you forgot what you fought for. You failed to understand why and how they colonized you. This is the way I see it. You will be born in Maphisa," Biko said with a hint of finality.

"Maphisa? Where is it?" Mugabe asked.

A number of people gave the answer in a chorus: "Maphisa is in Zimbabwe."

"In Matabeleland," Biko completed.

"But, but, must I go back to the earth?" Mugabe stammered.

"This is the judgment from the Eternal One," Equiano said.

"If I should go back to the earth, then please send me to Hong Kong."

"Why?" Equiano asked, smiling.

"I have a house and some money there. Not as much as other African leaders, though."

"Believe me, the Hong Kong people are smart. They have put your money to a better use."

"Then to Cuba? I have some money there, too. At least I will retrieve it for Zimbabwe."

"Too late. Fidel Castro cannot recognize you any more," Equiano went on. "Why wouldn't you go to Zimbabwe?"

"It is hell."

"Do you mean that Zimbabwe is hell?" a man's voice asked.

"Hell, that is Zimbabwe," responded Mugabe.

"We didn't think so," the judges said in a chorus.

"I know what I am talking about," Mugabe insisted. "Trust me."

"Oh, well, that is the verdict," Equiano said. "You should see it as an opportunity to grow." He knocked his gavel on the table for the last time, bringing the trial to an end.

◆◆

People gathered in groups to discuss the outcome of the trial. From their faces, it was obvious that they were satisfied with the verdict. After all, the Almighty thought the same way they did: Mugabe was headed to hell.

As they were still exchanging pleasantries and their impressions of the trial, the ceiling gradually split apart in two equal halves like the curtain of an opera stage. Two smiling angels sailed down, slowly, gracefully. One of them held a golden handcuff. They walked straight to Mugabe, who, as if defying the verdict handed down to him, sat on his chair in childish stubbornness. But the angels were unruffled, true to their nature. They calmly approached him, one to his left and the other to his right; they put their hands to his and frog-marched him out of his seat while his bodyguards looked on.

Mugabe wouldn't be Mugabe if he didn't put up a fight. This much we know. He did! And what a fight it was. So vigorous was it that one thought that the 84-year-old body had magically taken on the strength of a sumo wrestler. He flailed his hands and kicked his legs and scratched the angels, yelling: "Don't touch me. I am a victim. Zimbabwe is mine. I am a Zimbabwean. Zimbabwe for Zimbabweans. *Aluta continua.*"

But the angels were unfazed. With a feather-light ease, they latched their handcuffs on the old man's hands behind him and dragged him away while he screamed. People were surprised to see his excellency, one who used to howl like an African lion, now cry like a frightened child.

Footnote #6

Postcolonial Fever: mental disease. It is the condition of mental degradation rampant among the formerly colonized or oppressed people of the world.

Symptoms:

a) a belief by the victim that he or she has eyes in the back of his head and therefore he walks like a crab

b) state of paranoia that the world consists of strings of conspiracy against the victim and his people

c) the victim's unwillingness to emulate the path of progress from some other people; the victim sees this inability as being true to his roots

d) postcolonial fever is to *Guku* what pupa is to butterfly

e) the illusion that resistance *per se* is a virtue which implies the inability to transition to nation-building

Prolegomena to the Gukupedia: According to WMHO (World Mental Health Organization), quite a large number of the world population is exposed to *viridae postcolonitis* especially if they are naive enough to believe in the inviolability of the precepts of their religion and tradition, and, if they are too meek to challenge the wisdom of their elders. When they are infected, they are most likely to become knee-jerk reactionary moral phoneys. In the advanced stage of their infection, they experience fits of epileptic seizure during which they despise other people's object of symbolic relevance: institutions, artworks, food, books, flags, effigies of rulers, pictures of movie stars, even ideas; they spit and trample upon them in the belief that doing so solved their existential

Epilogue

And so, it came to be that, after six long, troubled hours of the night, Mugabe flailed his hands and kicked his legs, shouting hogwash. Stupefied by this sudden, unusual behavior from her dear husband of nearly two decades, Grace Mugabe reached for him: "My lord, my lord," she called in her singsong voice. "Wake up, my lord. What is wrong?"

Snapping at the air a few more times like a fish washed up to the strand, then yawning like a drowsy dog, Mugabe finally came to his senses. He looked left and right, glanced at his wrists and, surprised to see no handcuffs, turned to Grace. "I am sorry," he said, yawning, "I had a dreadful dream."

"Oh, we forgot to sprinkle the holy water yesterday," she blurted. "I should have said my full rosary."

"Did the pilot ever report any mechanical problems with the plane?"

"Yes, we had to turn back to the Egyptian airport. But it was repaired quickly."

"I dreamed that we had a plane crash."

"God forbid that you'll die, my lord."

"I stood on trial."

"Trial? Who on earth can ever put you on trial? God forbid."

"It's about *Gukurahundi*."

"But it's already forgotten. There is no evidence at all."

"There was evidence in God's Court."

"No, no one can put you on trial, my lord."

"I was sure I saw God."

"That was just a dream. No one can see God. He is invisible."

"Are you sure we are right in all this?"

"If we're not sure, who else can be?"

He hummed, and gazed at the ceiling.

"Don't ever give up power to Morgan Tsvangirai," Grace's voice broke in. He turned to her. "The British will use him to get you. Let him rot in the opposition. Give power to Perence Shiri. He will not allow any trial."

"Ah, that devil. How I hate him."

"The devil you know is better than Morgan Tsvangirai."

"How did I get myself into this? I should have known that this was inevitable."

"Don't look back, my lord. Remember the pillar of salt."

"Am I really Kurtz?"

"Who is Kurtz?"

"Never mind," he said and fell silent. Returning his gaze to the ceiling, he murmured to himself: "They caught Radovan Karadzic."

END

Sincere thanks to these writers and guardians of human rights:

Yvonne Vera, *Stone Virgins*

Dambudzo Marechera, *House of Hunger*

Chenjerai Hove, *Shebeen Tales: Messages from Harare*

Andrew Norman, *Robert Mugabe and the Betrayal of Zimbabwe*

Martin Meredith, *Our Votes, Our Guns: Robert Mugabe and the Tragedy of Zimbabwe.*

David Blair, *Degrees in Violence: Robert Mugabe and the Struggle for Power in Zimbabwe*

The Catholic Commission for Justice and Peace in Zimbabwe,

Gukurahundi in Zimbabwe: A Report on the Disturbances in Matabeleland and the Midlands 1980-1988

Jan Raath, "Robert Mugabe's militia burn opponent's wife alive" http://www.timesonline.co.uk/tol/news/world/africa/article4116638.ece

Gratitude

The author wishes to thank Mr. Walter Vogel for his friendship and support.

About the Author

Chielozona Eze is a Nigerian writer and philosopher. He studied Catholic theology, philosophy and literature, creative writing in Nigeria, Austria, Germany and the US. He is a Stellenbosch Fellow and the recipient of the Olaudah Equiano Prize for African Fiction. He teaches Postcolonial African Literature at Northeastern Illinois University, Chicago.

www.ingramcontent.com/pod-product-compliance
Lightning Source LLC
Chambersburg PA
CBHW050128030726
47505CB00007B/2093